FALLIN' FOR ANOTHER CHICK'S MAN

KEVINA HOPKINS

Fallin' For Another Chick's Man

Mailing List

To stay up to date on new releases, plus get information on contests, sneak peeks, and more,

Go To The Website Below...

www.colehartsignature.com

CHAPTER ONE
MERCEDES

The scent of weed instantly hit my nostrils as I walked into my sister's house. She and her boyfriend Bryce were throwing a tattoo party. It looked like everybody from the block was inside their crib. There was music blasting and people were sitting around playing games of spades. Looking around, I finally found Myra leaning against the wall talking to our brother, Montez .

As I was walking toward them, some guy grabbed me by my arm to get my attention.

"What's up ma, what's your name?" some dark-skin guy with yellow teeth asked.

I looked down at him and then at my arm before pulling away.

"I'm not interested," I told him the nicest way possible.

"Bitch, do you know who I am?" he yelled, getting the attention of the people around us.

"No nigga, do you know who the fuck I am?" I countered.

Before the dude got a chance to respond, my brother's fist was connecting to his jaw.

"Motherfucker, don't put your hands on her again, and she ain't no bitch," Montez bellowed.

"My fault Tez, I ain't know that was you," the guy mumbled.

"That's my lil' sister so you make sure you remember her face the next time you decide to be disrespectful," Montez said, pulling me close to him.

"Hey Tez, I could have handled him," I said, hugging my brother.

"I know you can, but you know as long as I'm around you never have to. I don't know why you have those lil' ass shorts on anyway. You about to stand by me all night," he replied, grabbing my hand and walking me over to our sister.

"Girl, you ain't been here five minutes and you already got shit jumping up," Myra laughed, leaning over to hug me.

"Shit, that wasn't my fault. That was that disrespectful ass nigga and your brother," I stated, eyeing Montez .

Montez was like a gentle giant. In the streets he was a giant and his name rang loud. When it came to me and Myra, he was as gentle as it came. He's there whenever we need him no matter what. You can't tell that man that we're not his daughters. He practically played the father role to me and my siblings for the past eight years while our father was locked up.

My father has five kids and four baby mamas. Montez is thirty, making him the oldest. Stephen is twenty-eight, Kiana is twenty-five, Myra is twenty-three, and I'm twenty-one. Even though most of us have different mothers, my father made sure that we all grew up together and had a close relationship with one another. I don't know how he did it, but all of our mothers got along. I wouldn't call them friends but they were all cordial for our sake. We didn't have to spend holidays or birthdays separately. When he got one of us he got all of us. We stayed that way until he was killed eight years ago in a drive-by shooting.

It was like once my father died, the link to the chain that was keeping me and my siblings together broke. Montez did his best to pick up where my father left off at, but at the time he was only twenty-two so there was only so much that he could do on his own. My brother Stephen was around when he wasn't out chasing females and doing dumb shit. Eventually the things he was doing caught up with him and he ended up in prison two years after my father passed for attempted murder. My sister Kiana went away to Florida State University. She stayed there for about a year and a half after graduation then came back acting like an entire different person, so we love her from a distance. As far as me and Myra goes, we remained close because we lived under the same roof since we had the same mother. We also have a younger brother named Marquis. He's thirteen years old but he has a different father than us.

"That was PJ, don't pay him no mind. He's harmless and now that Tez done stepped in you won't have to worry about him or any of the other niggas in here," Myra pointed out.

"It's cool, I'm not going to be here long anyway. I have to get back to the house with Kayla. Jermaine said he has some business to take care of tonight," I replied.

"Girl, what business does he have? Is he finally going out to get a damn job?" Myra asked.

"Myra, don't start, he's been looking," I advised her.

If it's not obvious by now, Myra doesn't like my boyfriend Jermaine. She hasn't liked him since day one and here it is almost four years later and she still doesn't hide it. She only tolerates him because of me and our daughter. If I'm being honest, at this point I only deal with him because of our daughter. If I didn't have a three-year-old child with him I probably would have been left. I got pregnant right before my eighteenth birthday and I didn't know shit about raising a baby, so I relied on Jermaine and his family.

When me and Myra was teenagers my mother used to always tell us don't go out and get pregnant because she's done raising her babies. We never knew what that really meant until Myra got pregnant when she was eighteen. My mother allowed her to stay home during the pregnancy but once the baby came, she had to find somewhere else to go. Luckily for her, she was able to get on low-income housing, which eventually turned into section eight, so she and my nephew were good.

You would've thought I would have learned from watching my mother kick Myra out that I wouldn't follow in her footsteps, but I did. A year later I ended up pregnant and in the same predicament as her. Only I wasn't able to get housing as quick as she did, so I ended up moving in with Jermaine and his mother until we were able to find our own place. Don't get me wrong now, my mother loves her grandkids. She practically has both of them every weekend if she doesn't have plans and she makes sure they have everything they need. I guess her kicking us out was her doing tough parenting. I just know that if my daughter ever gets pregnant while she's still living with me, a roof will remain over her head, but to each its own.

"Girl whatever, I just know next month you better be ready for my birthday trip to Miami. Ma is watching the kids and Montez already paid for everything for you so you don't have no excuse not to come. That nigga will be okay by himself for a weekend."

"I already told you that I'll be there, Myra. You don't have to worry about that."

"Good, because it's going to be a trip you won't forget." Myra smiled, causing me to smile as well.

This was definitely going to be a much-needed trip, even if it was only going to be for a weekend. I can't remember the last time I went on a kid-free vacation. I love being a mother but at the same time, I'm young so I want to live life to the fullest. I'm a mother first then a bad bitch immediately afterward.

I stayed at the gathering chilling with my sister and brother for a couple hours until Jermaine started blowing up my phone. I was going to get a tattoo but there were too many people in front of me. I didn't want to make Jermaine late for whatever it was he had to do so I left and headed home. I parked in front of our apartment complex and headed inside the building.

I held my breath as I walked upstairs to the second floor. There was always the scent of piss and ammonia mixed together in the hallway. I can't wait until I can get on my feet to find somewhere else to live. It's a roof over my head and something that I can call my own so I can't complain too much.

Grabbing my keys from my purse, I used them to enter my house. As soon as I stepped foot in there I wanted to walk back out. The living room was messy as hell, like always. It's not a day that goes by that doesn't involve me having to clean up. There were toys all over the place and beer bottles on the table. Whenever Jermaine watched Kayla he allowed her to do whatever she wanted to do.

"What took you so long to get here? I told you I have shit to do," Jermaine complained, walking into the living room.

"I was only gone for three hours," I replied, looking down at my watch. It wasn't even eleven yet and the nigga was acting like I had been out all night.

"That's not what I'm talking about. I talked to you thirty minutes ago and you said you were leaving then. It only takes twenty minutes to get here from your sister's house."

"Are you serious right now? I stopped at the gas station to get some gas and something to drink. Do you have the money for the light bill?" I asked, changing the subject because I hate when he does this. He always wants to know what I'm doing every minute of the day but let me call and ask where he at, he acts like I asked him for his social security number.

"I don't have it right now but I should have it in the morning. That's why I'm trying to go out now to make some moves to get some money."

"Maine, that's the same thing you've been saying all week. The lights are already a month behind. You know my lights can't get disconnected or they'll take my voucher away," I reminded him.

"If you can't be patient, get the money from your brother. If he would have put me on like I asked him to we wouldn't even be having the problems we're having right now. We could be living in a nice ass crib like his. That nigga selfish as fuck if you ask me. If I was getting the kind of money he got, my baby sister wouldn't be living in the gutter broke. I'd make sure to look out for you and the rest of my family."

"Well it's good thing that nobody asked you. It's not my brother's responsibility to take care of me and my baby. I'm not sharing a bed with him every night and he doesn't sleep under this roof. He don't have to put you on if he don't want to. You're a grown ass man looking for a handout from another man. That says more about you as a man than my brother," I spat.

I played about a lot of things, but my brother wasn't one of them. When Montez found out I was pregnant he offered to move me in with him or get me a place of my own. The only thing about that though was that Jermaine wasn't going to be able to live with me. My brother was willing to take care of me and Kayla but he wasn't about to take care of a grown ass man.

I couldn't be mad at him for that because Jermaine should be man enough to take care of his family on his own.

"Watch your motherfucking mouth before I hit your ass in it."

"Jermaine, I advise you to walk out of this house like you had planned because we both know you don't want those kinds of problems."

"What you gone do? Call your brother? You think when they made his gun they stopped making others?" he questioned, walking up in my face.

I took a step back because if his crazy ass put his hands on me, we were about to be rumbling in this bitch.

"That liquor you was drinking must've gave you some real courage because we both know Montez is not to be played with. Since you look like you're kind of drunk, I'm going to let the slick shit you talking slide today," I informed him, handing him the keys to my car since his was fucked up.

He got into a car accident a couple months ago and totaled it out. Unfortunately, he didn't have car insurance and no money to get a new one. If Montez knew I was letting him drive the Benz he bought me, he'd have a fit. He hated Jermaine more than Myra did. He mainly hated him because he thought he wasn't good enough for me, which was probably true but it was too late now. I fell in love with this nigga and gave him a baby.

"You know you only talking like this because I ain't got money. When I had money your ass was willing to do any and everything for a nigga. It's cool though, because I'll be back on my shit soon and you'll be back to worshipping the ground I walk on."

"Well how about you get some then we can test that theory," I responded sarcastically.

Jermaine gave me a look like he wanted to slap the fuck out

of me, but he knew better. We argued all the time but it never got physical. Well, he'll snatch my ass up or push me out of the way, but that's as far as it goes. He knows the minute he physically put his hands on me to do bodily harm is the minute he's going to make my daughter a fatherless child. I don't believe in that domestic shit. If I don't put my hands on him he doesn't have a right to put his on me.

"Don't wait up," he said, snatching the keys from me and heading for the front door.

"I didn't intend on it," I mumbled, dropping my purse on the couch.

I walked to my daughter's bedroom to look in on her. She was laying in her bed, knocked out sleep. I kissed her on the forehead then closed the door behind me. Jermaine might be a shitty boyfriend at times but he was a great father to Kayla. He made sure that she was good at all times. I just wished he was able to help out more financially.

I'm trying my best to be patient with Jermaine because he is a good man and it wasn't always like this between us. When I first met him I was seventeen years old and he was twenty-one. I was a big girl so I wasn't used to getting attention like my sisters, friends, or the girls from my school. I was insecure as hell and my mindset was fucked up.

It was like I knew I had a pretty face but that wasn't enough for the guys my age. They wanted the picture-perfect female, so when Maine approached me at the corner store I was ecstatic. At the time, I was so damn naive that it made no sense. I was inexperienced and never had gotten real attention like that from a guy before

I didn't realize that even though I was big I was still beautiful. I didn't know my worth so all it took was for the first boy to show me some attention. I didn't think about the fact that I had no business being in this twenty-one-year-old man's face.

All it took was for him to tell me I was pretty. Next thing I know, I'm going to his house to chill with him a few days later. One thing led to another and that same night I was giving him my virginity.

After the first night we had sex we built a secret relationship. He convinced me that we couldn't go out in public because I was underage. Me not knowing no better, I agreed because I didn't want him to get in trouble because of me. Myra was the only one that knew about my relationship with Jermaine because I tell her everything, and I didn't know anything about sex so who better to ask than my big sister. As soon as I told her about him she told me to abort mission because he was only using me for sex. By that time I was too far gone and wasn't trying to hear what she was talking about, so I continued seeing him, I just didn't tell her about it.

It wasn't until I got pregnant that I told my family about him. His mother was the only person that knew about me at the time because he was still living with her. That should have been the first red flag for me. I mean, what twenty-one-year-old man was still living at home with his mother willingly? He had a job working at a warehouse so he made enough money to get a decent one-bedroom apartment for himself.

We lived with his mother until our daughter Makayla turned one, then we moved into our own two-bedroom apartment. Everything was going great because we both were working so we were able to afford rent, bills, and live comfortably. All of that changed last year when Jermaine's job laid him off. Instead of him going to find another job, he decided he wanted to be a dope boy, knowing damn well he ain't know shit about selling drugs. Then he had the nerve to ask my brother to put him on, and Tez told him no because he'd hate to have to kill his niece's father. He wasn't about to let him play with his product.

CHAPTER TWO

JERMAINE

I've been sitting with my niggas for the past hour now feeling chill and having a good ass time drinking and passing blunts back and forth. Music blasting and bad bitches everywhere. This is definitely what I needed after spending the whole day babysitting. Don't get me wrong now. I love the hell out of my daughter but she's super active and can be a handful.

I told Mercedes ass to put her in daycare. She has me feeling like I'm a bitch or some shit. I ain't no damn stay at home mama. Talking about why should she pay for daycare when I'm at home not doing shit anyway? I asked her ass now what if I was out working or found a new job, then what. Her reply was then she'd put her in daycare because I'd have money to pay for it.

It's like ever since I lost my job and she's lost weight, little slick shit has been coming out of her mouth. If I didn't know any better, I'd think she was getting herself together to leave my ass. I ain't worried about it though. I'm the first nigga Mercedes has ever been with and she belongs to me. I love her but I need to knock her off that pedestal she's been climbing on lately, because I don't give a fuck what she or her family thinks, I'm still a man. I'm having a rough time right now but hopefully, this meeting I have tonight goes as planned, then I'll be back on my feet and she'll be back worshipping the ground I walk on.

Mercedes is a good woman and I love her. She gave me a beautiful daughter and she has a heart of gold. I know most of the things she's feeling right now is my fault because I haven't been doing my part. I tried finding another nine to five but I didn't want to be in no hot ass warehouse again. I wanted to make more money so that I could find a house for me and my family. I watched movies and saw how my niggas was pushing drugs and getting major bags. I figured I could do the same thing with the right connections. Had Montez looked out for me when I asked we'd be living in a nice ass crib right now and money wouldn't be an option.

I swear I don't get niggas like him. His ass is rich and his sister is struggling. He's refusing to help her for whatever reason that I can't understand. He buys her and Makayla expensive shit all the time but he doesn't give her money. Take the Benz she's driving for instance. He bought it brand-new off the show room for her twenty-first birthday a few months ago and pays for the insurance for it. I thought that was the dumbest shit ever because that car don't put food in our house or pay the bills. He could have got her a simple used car and gave her the rest of the money to do whatever she wanted with it. When I suggested that to her she told me to mind my business, so I left it alone.

Me and the guys hung out for a little while longer until it was time for our meeting. If the meeting is scheduled for two in the morning you can tell it's some shady shit going on. At this point I didn't give a fuck because I need the money. I'm going to get it and then flip it. I want to show Montez that I didn't need his ass. I was going to make him regret not adding me to his team because I was now going to be his competition.

After a twenty-minute drive, we pulled up to the address and I parked out front. I double checked that I had the correct address because from the outside it looked like an auto body shop. The address was correct so me and the guys got out of the car. I knocked on the door then a couple minutes later, a husky guy came and opened the door for us.

As we walked in I took a look at my surroundings. It was definitely an auto shop but I'm sure it was just a front. We walked further inside then entered a door that led to a long hall. We followed behind the guy until he abruptly stopped at a door, almost causing me to bump into him. The nigga had the nerve to look at me crazy as if it wasn't his fault.

We entered the office where Meech was sitting at a table smoking a blunt. He nodded his head at us without saying a word as we took a seat at the table with him. Meech was a dark-skinned, fat nigga in his midfifties with a mouth full of gold. He was getting money and he didn't try to hide it. He's on the same level as Montez and from what I heard, they have some sort of beef going on right now.

The last thing I wanted to do was go against Mercedes and her family but Tez left me no choice. I just had to make sure this didn't get back to Mercedes first because I know she'll tell her brother. She's loyal to me by default but her brother comes before me. I know if she had to pick a side it would never be mine. Unfortunately, I don't have time to worry about those consequences right now.

I ran into my cousin Kelvin the other day and I told him about my financial situation. He told me he could set up a meeting with his boss for me that would have a major payout. I agreed without knowing who his boss was. At the time the only thing I heard was payout. I didn't know what the hell I was going to have to do or who I was doing it with. It wasn't until yesterday I found out the meeting was with Meech. By then it was too late because I had no other alternative. At first I was going to cancel it because I know working with Meech was going to bring more problems my way, but then I was like fuck it. I don't owe Tez shit because he ain't never did anything for me.

"What's up Meech, I'm Maine, this is Rob and Don," I introduced us.

"What's up, these are the only two in your crew? You think you can pull this off with just the three of you?" he inquired.

A confused look spread across my face because I didn't know what he was talking about when he said my crew. I thought this was going to be about a drug transaction and me working for him.

"Pull what off?" I asked, finally confused.

"Kev didn't tell you what the job was going to be?" he asked.

"Nah, he just said you agreed to meet with me."

"Okay, I need you to rob this nigga Tez for me. I've been trying to find out where he lives but I haven't had any luck. All I know is that he has a trap in Union City. They're going to have a block party tonight around seven. I want you to get rid of his homie. Once he's out of the way then it'll be easier to get to Tez."

"Okay, I can do that." I nodded my head in agreement even though I was ready to shit bricks. I was only expecting to sell drugs and maybe have to do it on Tez's turf. I didn't think I was going to have to play a part in my girl's brother's death. If anything ever happened to Tez, it would devastate Mercedes. Now I had to make sure that Meech didn't find out that I knew Montez personally. The funny thing about knowing Tez

personally is that I don't know where he lays his head. That's
been some top secret shit ever since I've been with Mercedes.
The only people that knows where he really lives is his family,
and their lips are sealed.

"Cool, come back Sunday night to collect thirty-five thousand each," he said.

"Thirty-five thousand each?" I repeated, making sure I
heard him right.

"Yeah, if you pull this off you'll each get thirty-five thousand and there will be more where this comes from."

"Okay, we'll take care of it," I assured him, getting up from
the table with my guys following behind me. After hearing I
could make thirty-five thousand dollars just from doing one
job, all doubts went out the window. I had never seen that
much money at one time. This was the kind of money I was
hoping for when I joined the drug business.

We silently walked back to the car and as soon as I pulled
off, Don spoke up.

"Nigga, I know you not about to play a part in setting your
girl's brother up?"

"Shit, did you hear the part where we're each getting
thirty-five thousand dollars apiece for this? Do you know what
we could do with that kind of money? All we have to do is do
this one thing for him and then we're in. We can make enough
money and put it all together then start working for ourselves
long before it comes down to having to kill Tez."

"Man, all money ain't good money, and did you forget the
fact that we ain't killers?" Don asked.

"We don't have to be killers. We can pull one of the young
niggas in from the block and let them pull the trigger. We can
each give him five thousand of our cut. He don't have to know
how much we're being paid," I suggested, hoping this would
shut they asses up. I ain't never killed anybody either and I

have the most to lose, but they don't see me sitting here bitching.

"I don't know Maine, I need to think about this. Selling drugs is one thing but murder is on an entire different level," Don replied.

Hearing him say he was going to have to think about it was his way of saying he wasn't going to do it. I couldn't make him and I damn sure wasn't about to beg him to help out. He was a grown ass man and if he wanted to miss out on this kind of money, that was on him.

"Okay, what about you Rob? You've been quiet since you got in the car," I questioned.

"I'm just sitting here thinking. That's a hell of a lot of money and it can go a long way. Shit, this will be fucking over your people, and if you cool with it then I'm cool with it too," he stated, shrugging.

"My nigga," I said, nodding my head. Rob has always been a grimy ass nigga. That's one of the reasons why I kept him close by. He was the one willing to do the shit that we wouldn't do.

Thirty minutes later I pulled up to Don's house. I was glad that Rob's car was there because I didn't feel like driving across town to drop him off. We lit up another blunt and chilled for a minute. My cell phone vibrated in my pocket. Looking up at the dashboard, I saw it was three thirty. I thought it was Mercedes calling to see where I was but it was a text from this chick Tori.

Tori: *I miss you daddy, when am I going to get a chance to see you?*

Me: *I can be there in twenty.*

Tori: *Okay, I'll be waiting.*

"Yo, I'm out," I said, starting the car up.

"Wifey told you bring your ass home?" Rob asked.

"Nah, Mercedes hasn't even called or text me since I left. That was Tori."

"Yeah, you gone need this money because Mercedes is going to fuck around and kick your ass out when she finds out."

"I ain't worried about her finding out. I've got away with it all this time. Tori not going to say anything. She knows how to play her part," I spoke confidently because I was. Me and Tori had an understanding and I wasn't worried about her telling Mercedes anything.

I drove away and headed in the direction of Tori's house even though I should have been taking my ass home. I hadn't seen her in a couple weeks and I was in need of busting a nut. Mercedes been acting like she can't break a nigga off. I guess since we've been arguing damn near every day for the past two weeks she feels like I don't deserve none. Shit, I'm not about to beg her for none when there's another bitch willingly throwing the pussy to me every chance she gets.

Pulling up to Tori's house, I sent her a text letting her know that I was outside. I parked and waited outside the car until she appeared in the doorway wearing a silk robe. I took the couple steps to her door then followed her to her bedroom. As soon as the door was closed I embraced her in a long hug before kissing her on the lips and taking a step back.

I couldn't help but admire her beauty. She had a mocha complexion and couldn't weigh no more than one hundred forty pounds with brown eyes. She wasn't tall or short. She was more on the average height. I met her about six months ago at her job when I went to switch out my phone service. She was one of the customer service representatives. She showed me the phones then signed me up for new service. We had small talk while we waited and before I left, we exchanged phone numbers. After that we linked up and we've been fucking around ever since.

"I missed you, baby," she said, dropping her robe.

"I missed you too, ma," I replied, pulling her close to me, latching my lips onto hers.

We shared a deep kiss before I gently placed her on the bed. I undressed then climbed in with her. Trailing kisses down her body, I stopped when I made it to her inner thighs, inhaling her sweet nectar before placing my tongue on her pussy, causing her to jerk. She softly moaned as I gently nibbled on her clit.

"Fuck," she moaned, grabbing onto the back of my head, pushing it further into her. I sucked her clit, feeling her juices drip down my chin. I made sure to lick every drop before latching my lips back onto her pussy. She tried pushing my head away but I wouldn't budge, grabbing onto her thighs tightly to keep her in place. After making her come a second time I released my grip and hovered over her, kissing her on the lips sloppily, allowing her to taste herself.

Breaking the kiss, I rolled over onto my back and she wasted no time placing the tip of my dick in her mouth, causing pre-cum to ooze out. My dick was already erect from eating her pussy. I loved pleasing a woman and giving head. That alone made my dick get hard faster than getting it sucked.

Inch by inch, she took me deeper into her mouth until I was reaching the back of her throat. Her gag reflexes was out of this world. Rubbing my fingers through her hair, I began bobbing her head up and down. She was swirling her tongue as she picked up the pace, causing me to groan. I could feel myself about to cum and I was on a time limit, so I gently pushed her head away, indicating for her to stop.

"Sit on it for me," I ordered.

Like the good girl that she was, she simply obliged. Placing her hands onto my chest, she gently slid down my dick. He pussy wrapped around it, making hard for me not to nut in her. Her shit was wet as hell and I can't get enough of it. Once she was adjusted she slowly started riding me. Holding onto her waist, I made sure she was feeling every inch of me. She bit down on her lip before throwing her head back. The way she was moaning and groaning, I could tell she was loving every bit of it.

"F-fuck, you about to make me cum," she moaned as I picked up the pace.

"Cum on this dick then. Let me feel you," I groaned.

It only took about two minutes before she was cumming all over my dick. Flipping her over on her back, I lifted her leg over my shoulder and plunged my dick inside of her. She was getting loud as hell and I didn't want her waking her parents, so I placed my hand over her mouth to muffle her sounds.

I took my time stroking her, making sure to hit her spot each time until she was squirting everywhere. I loved the way her body reacted to me whenever we fucked. I had let her get a few nuts off but now it was time for me to get mine. Pulling out of her, she knew what time it was. She turned over, getting on all fours, making the perfect arch in her back to give me a perfect view of her ass.

I got behind her, placing one hand on her waist and using the other one to slide my dick back inside of her. We both winced as I beat away at her flesh. She buried her head in the pillow as she cried out my name.

"Oh my god baby, what are you doing. That feels so fucking good," she cried.

"Throw that ass back for me. Take all of this dick," I demanded, slapping her on the ass. Her rhythm matched my strokes as I blew her back out.

"Shit, I'm about to cum again," she panted.

"Me too," I announced.

I waited until I felt her juices run down my dick before I pulled out and nutted on her ass. I fell back on my back, trying to catch my breath for a minute. Tori slid next to me, placing her head on my chest. I looked over at the clock and saw that it was almost six. I needed to go but at the same time, I didn't want it to seem like I was just fucking her then leaving. Typically I tried to stay with her for at least thirty minutes, but her parents would be up soon and I didn't want them to see me sneaking out.

"Thank you for coming to see me. I really did miss you. I didn't think you were going to be able to come out this late," she told me, breaking the silence.

"Girl, I ain't got no damn curfew. I told you that I only live with my baby mama because of our daughter. We don't even sleep in the same room together. With the work schedule that she has she's barely at home, so it's easier to be there to watch my baby while she's at work."

"Okay, well y'all are going to have to figure out a new arrangement because I'm pregnant. I'm still living with my parents and you're living with another woman. I think it's time that we get our own place together. Besides, I'm not that comfortable with you living with her anymore. I was fine with it at first because we weren't serious, but now it's a different story. I'm not saying that I don't trust you. It's just I know females can be on some sneaky shit," she explained.

I was stuck on the fact that she was pregnant. I had really fucked up this time. Tori was just someone to have fun with. Don't get me wrong, she's a cool chick and I like spending time with her, but I don't love her. My heart is with Mercedes I don't see how that will ever change. Now I have to try to figure out how to lie my way out of this situation and make sure Cedes never finds out about this. Between getting someone else pregnant and working with her brother's opp, she'll never forgive me.

"How far along are you?" I asked after the awkward silence.

"I'm two months and before you ask, yes, I'm keeping it. I'm twenty-six years old so I think it's an appropriate time for me to have a baby. We love each other so I don't see what the problem is."

"I never said it was a problem, baby. I just wanted to know how far along you were. You don't have to worry about anything. We can work on getting a place together. Start looking up some spots and we can go check them out."

"Okay, I'm so excited to see what's in store for our future." She smiled.

Seeing her excited and smiling like that made me feel like shit. The last thing I wanted to do was break this girl's heart. On the other hand, I might not have to break her heart and I'll have no choice but to move in with her, because if Cedes finds out my ass is going to be homeless. I just hope it doesn't affect the relationship I have with my daughter.

"I'm looking forward to our future as well. I need to be heading out though, before your parents wake up."

"Alright, I can't wait until the day comes where you won't have to sneak in and out. I want to be the first face you see when you wake up in the morning and the last you see at night," she said, climbing out of bed.

I climbed out of bed behind her and put my clothes on. I never knew she felt like this because we never discussed a future. I guess I should have known better since we've been fucking for six months. She's told me she loved me multiple times and I've lied saying I love her too because I didn't know what else to tell her.

"Bae, do you have two hundred dollars I can borrow until

Monday morning? I'm locked out of my bank account and I have to go into the branch to gain access," I lied.

"Sure, I know you're good for it," she replied, walking over to grab her purse. She looked inside, grabbing her wallet, then handed me two crisp hundred-dollar bills.

"Thanks ma, I appreciate it," I stated, grabbing the money.

"You're welcome, bae."

We walked down the stairs and she led the way to the front door. I gave her a kiss on the lips before walking outside to the car. Basically, my entire situation with Tori is based off of a lie. She doesn't know that I'm still in a relationship with Mercedes and she doesn't know that I'm broke. I told her I do freelance work for a construction company. She also thinks Mercedes' Benz is mine. I've been able to make enough hustling here and there to take her on dates. She's not hard to please so it doesn't take a lot of money to do that.

I got in the car and drove home. There was no need to rush because it was already early. I got the money from Tori, so hopefully when I give that to Mercedes she'll believe my lie about being out working.

I parked in front of the building then headed upstairs. I unlocked the door and slightly closed it, not trying to make much noise. I walked quietly through the house and to the kitchen to get something to drink. As I opened the refrigerator, I heard Mercedes clear her throat, causing me to jump.

"Where the fuck have you been at all night?" she asked.

"I was out handling business. Here's the money for the lights," I said, handing her the money.

"Do you think I'm stupid, Jermaine? You smell like a bitch. You was out all this time and couldn't wash your ass first?"

"Come on now Mercedes, how the hell was I out cheating when I just brought you money for the bill? Everything I do is never good enough for your ass," I spat.

"Motherfucker, you not about to flip the script or make me feel bad, with your dumb ass. This not the first night, well day, you done came home smelling like another woman. I just chose not to say anything, but bet. I'm glad to know this the game we playing," she said before walking away.

I didn't even bother following her because when she got like this it wasn't shit I could say or do to calm her down. I went straight to the bathroom and took a quick shower. Once I was done, I climbed in bed and went to sleep.

CHAPTER THREE
MERCEDES

I laid silently pretending I was sleep as Jermaine climbed in bed. Once he started snoring I got out. I was disgusted and didn't want to sleep near him. He expects me to believe he was out hustling until seven in the morning. He could've come up with a better lie.

Climbing out of bed, I walked over to the dresser and picked up his wallet. Opening it, I only saw a twenty-dollar bill. There was no way in hell he had been hustling all night and only made two hundred twenty dollars. He was with some bitch and she gave him the money. I wasn't going to be dumb and give it back because the bill needed to be paid and I was tired of spending my own money on all the bills. I also wasn't 'bout to play these games with him. I was so pissed that I couldn't even go back to sleep.

I took a shower and got dressed in a pair of black leggings with a white t-shirt and a pair of white Ones. I than went into my daughter's room and woke her up. Jermaine had already bathed her last night so I just had to get her dressed and comb her hair.

It took an hour for me to get her all the way together before I grabbed my keys and left the house. It was still early so I drove to Ihop for us to have breakfast. I sat enjoying my time with my baby. I tried helping her eat because she was making a mess but she wouldn't let me. She was a very independent child for her age. I guess it was a good thing since school would be starting for her soon. She was going to go to school from eight to twelve and then daycare after that. I was tired of hearing Jermaine's ass cry about watching his own fucking daughter.

Once we finished breakfast, I left to go to my sister Myra's house. I know she's probably still sleeping but I need my big sister right now. She might fuss but she's going to be there for me regardless. It took me about twenty minutes to get to her. I parked in front of her house then helped my daughter out before going to ring the bell.

It took a few minutes before the front door opened. Myra looked like she was ready to curse me out until she saw Makayla standing with me. My sister might act ratchet but when it came to the kids, it was a different story.

"B.I.T.C.H. you better be lucky you got my niece with you knocking on the door this early," she said, spelling out the word bitch.

"I know, I'm sorry. Jermaine pissed me off and I didn't know where to go," I responded, walking in the house.

"Did y'all eat already?" she asked.

"Yeah, we just left Ihop."

"Good, because I didn't feel like cooking. Go take her to Melanie's room so we can talk," Myra instructed.

"Okay," I replied, sitting my purse down on the couch.

I led Kayla to my niece's room and turned on cartoons for her. As long as cartoons was on she'd be good. She was most likely going to fall right back to sleep since I woke her up anyway. I cracked the door behind me as I left the room, heading back to the living room where Myra was sitting on the couch rolling a blunt. I wasn't sure if she had even eaten anything today yet but I wasn't one to judge because I needed to get high to clear my mind.

"So, what has Jermaine done this time?" Myra asked, getting straight to the point.

"Girl, so yesterday when I made it to the house his ass was tripping, talking about what took me so long to get home from your house. After that I asked him about the light money and that shit led to an argument. He claimed he was going out to take care of some business but didn't show up back home until almost seven this morning. He gave me the money for the light bill but he smelled like a bitch. I called him out on it and of course, he lied. Then he had the nerve to shower and get in the bed like nothing happened. I was so pissed I got out of bed to check his wallet and it was only twenty dollars in there. That's when I got dressed and left the house before I ended up catching a case."

"How the fuck is that nigga broke and cheating all at the same time? You're practically taking care of him and he can't keep his dick in his pants? You need to leave his ass and let Tez buy a house for you and Kayla. Shit, if it's about the dick there's plenty more of that out here," she replied.

"It's not about the dick, Myra. I still love him and he's the father of my child. He's been there for me for all of the ups and downs."

"So fucking what, you've more than paid for all of that shit this past year. Loving his broke ass is not going to keep that roof over you and my niece's head. There's so much better that could be going on with your life and you're letting him hold you back."

There wasn't much I could say to what Myra was saying

because it was the truth. I was bringing all of this shit on my own. I definitely had to sit down and reevaluate my life choices.

"You're right, I'm going to figure it out."

"Good, I don't know why niggas lie so much. I swear it don't make no damn sense. I'm starting to think Adam ate the apple and blamed it on Eve," Myra joked.

"Yeah, that's probably why they have that Adam's apple stuck in they throat," I laughed.

That was one thing I could count on Myra for. No matter what the situation was she was going to find a way to lighten the mood.

"Are you going to Tez's block party tonight?" Myra asked, changing the subject.

"I don't know. You know I don't be out there like that," I replied.

"Girl, you're only twenty-one years old and you be acting like a grandma. You need to get cute and come out. It'll be fun and you need to live a little. I'm sure Ma will watch Kayla for you, and if she can't Bryce's mother will watch her. You know she loves Kayla the same as she loves Melanie."

"Okay, I'll see what Ma says. I didn't bring anything out with me to wear so that means I'll have to go home, and I'm not trying to see Jermaine's face."

"Call Tez's ass and tell him to send you some money so you can go shopping for tonight. You already know he'll send it to you. I'm going to go throw on some clothes and get some money from Bryce, then we can go," she said, getting up from the couch.

I thought about it for a minute before dialing Tez's number.

"What's up, sis?" Tez answered on the third ring.

"Hey big head, what you doing?" I asked.

"About to handle some business in a minute. What's going on?"

"I'm at Myra's house right now and I was trying to find out if you can send me some money so I can buy something to wear tonight to your block party."

"Aight, I'm about to Zelle you now," he replied without hesitation.

"Thank you, big brother. I love you."

"I love you too, baby girl. I'll see you tonight," he told me before hanging up.

Two minutes later I got a Zelle notification on my phone. Tez had sent me five hundred dollars. This was something that he always did. I could ask him for fifty dollars and he'll send two hundred instead. This was definitely going to come in handy though. This was enough for my outfit, shoes, and some hair so Myra could do my hair. I called my mother and asked if she would watch Kayla tonight and she suggested I bring her right now. Everything Kayla would need was already at my mother's house, so I didn't have to worry about stopping to get her anything. She had turned me and Myra's room into our kids' room.

Forty minutes later, Myra came walking back in the living room in the same attire as me. I went in the back and got Kayla then we got in my car and left. Myra always acted like she couldn't drive and she had a new car just like me. Well, her car is a few years old now because Tez bought her a brand-new BMW for her twenty-first birthday. That was the car she wanted so that's what he got her.

I pulled up to my mother's house and sighed when I saw her boyfriend Dion's car in the driveway. Lord knows I can't stand that nigga. Hopefully he doesn't say anything to me out of pocket because I'm not in the mood today. I'll really give him a piece of my mind without sparing his feelings.

Climbing out of the car, I grabbed Kayla's hand and Myra followed behind me. I used my key to unlock my mother's three-bedroom home. I was hoping I could get in and get out without having to see Dion's face, but today just wasn't my day. His ass was sitting on the couch drinking a beer like it wasn't twelve o'clock in the afternoon. His ass was just as bad as Jermaine. That's probably why I didn't like his ass. I was starting to think me and my mama got the same taste in men.

I quickly shook that thought away because my daddy was far from a bitch nigga. He probably didn't know how to stay with the same woman at long periods of time, but he was a provider. None of us never went without when my father was here. He busted his ass to take care of all of his kids and made sure all of us had the best education. It was on us for how we turned out right now and the stupid decisions we made, because we wasn't raised like that. Things would be so different right now if my father was still here. I miss him more and more every day because he was my rock. I have to give it to Montez for stepping up in his place.

Looking at Dion sitting on the couch made me want to go and reevaluate my life even more. God knows I love my mother, but I didn't want to end up like her. She was the type of woman that didn't know how to be alone. It was like she needed a man just as much as she needed oxygen to breathe. It didn't matter what kind of man it was as long as it was a man. It was like after things didn't work out between her and my father, she got desperate and started doing dumb shit.

My mother was bringing all different kinds of men home with her, then she fucked around and got pregnant with my brother. That shit was embarrassing as hell because she didn't even know who his father was. She had to get a DNA test on three different men. The good thing about that was the baby was by a man with money and not one of the many alcoholics she dated. Marquis's father is actually in his life and has him more than my mother does, so he doesn't pay child support. He just gives her money toward the bills since the house is already paid off, courtesy of my father.

Dion looked our way before placing his attention back on the TV.

"Mona, your fast ass daughters are here and they used a key again," he yelled.

"Stop all that damn yelling, Dion. I told you that they don't have to knock on the door," my mother replied.

"I told you that they do. They don't pay no bills up in here," he said.

"What bills is it that you pay?" Myra inquired.

"Girl, don't worry about what bills I pay. Stay out of grown folks business," he slurred.

I was about to respond when Marquis came walking in the room. I embraced him in a long hug. Even though he was only thirteen years old, he was almost the same height as me. He was going to be taller than me and Myra. He got that from his father's side because my mother was only 5'5. Unfortunately, Myra took after her height. I was lucky to have a couple more inches over them, standing at 5'7.

"Marquis, did you clean your room like I asked you to? I left a plate in the microwave for you and your dad will be here in an hour, so you need to have your stuff together," my mother rattled off.

"Do I have to go right now? What you just say? I wanted to spend time with Kayla," he replied.

My little brother loved being an uncle. He was crazy about and Kayla and Melanie. He was always having his dad give him money to buy them stuff, and whenever he came back he had some kind of gift for them.

"Lil' nigga, you heard your mama. Go eat and clean that room so your ass can go," Dion yelled.

"Don't talk to my brother like that. Just because you with my mama don't give you no authority around here. You ain't none of our fathers," I pointed out.

"Girl, you better watch your mouth. I'm not none of your little friends. I'll beat your ass," he threatened.

"Dion, don't threaten my child. You're not going to do anything to her," my mother added.

"Nah, don't tell him shit. The minute he put his hands on me is the minute you're not going to have a boyfriend anymore because I won't hesitate to call my brother," I said.

"Just ignore him, Mercedes. It doesn't have to come down to that. Leave Kayla here and go enjoy your day," my mother replied, trying to resolve the issue. She knew that Montez didn't play when it came to me. He already had to come here once to handle one of my mother's boyfriends when I was younger and she didn't want that to happen again.

"Call your brother if you want to. His ass gone end up lying next to your daddy fucking with me," he stated.

No lie, hearing him say that struck a nerve. He could talk all the shit he wanted about me, but I didn't play when it came to my daddy. His death still fucked with my head to this day because he was supposed to had been taking me and Myra to the show that night. I never properly healed from that shit because the bullet that hit him wasn't even meant for him. My father didn't fuck with nobody. He used to be in the streets but by that time he was legit with a construction company and his own music studio.

Without hesitation, Myra ran over, hitting Dion straight in the face. She kept throwing hands and he tried getting her off of him. It took me and Mama to get her up off that man. I guess he got tired of her hitting him because he slapped her. That's when I jumped in and took over where she left off at. He really had life fucked up right now. Me and Myra were both tag teaming his ass at this point.

"Would you two stop! Y'all scaring Makayla," my mama yelled, getting my attention. I was so engrossed in what was going on with Dion that I didn't even hear my baby crying. Me and Myra immediately stopped, looking in the direction of my baby.

"Don't you ever in your fucking life fix your lips to threaten my brother or bring my father up. Your ass could never be half the man that either of them are," I spat, stepping away to get my baby.

"Let's go Cedes, and get Kayla. Bryce's mom can watch her today," Myra suggested, pulling out her phone.

"Come on now, y'all are being dramatic. I told you that I would watch my grandbaby so leave her here," my mother said.

"It's not about that, Ma. I don't trust leaving her here today after what just happened while he is here," I replied.

I walked in the back to tell my brother bye and my mother followed behind me.

"What is the issue between you and Dion? You're always starting a fight when he's here."

"I always start a fight? Did you not see what just took place in the living room? He was disrespectful to Marquis and my father. Not to mention he threatened Tez. He better be lucky it was me and Myra on his ass and I didn't call Tez instead," I pointed out.

"He didn't mean any harm by any of that. He's been having a rough couple of days. Please don't call your brother. I'll talk to Dion about it later. I need you to try and get along with him though because he's moving in. He asked me to marry him and

I said yes. I love him baby and I deserve the chance at happiness," she replied.

"You're right, Ma. Congratulations," I said, hugging her before going in my brother's room. I gave him a hug and promised to come get him once he comes back from his dad's house.

I left my brother's room and grabbed my daughter then we left out of the house. I couldn't wait to tell Myra what my mother had just told me.

"Bernice said she'll watch Kayla for you. We can take her over there now and continue on with our day as planned. We don't have to let what just happened ruin our day," Myra stated once we were in the car.

I nodded my head and drove off in the direction of Bernice's house. I was itching to tell Myra what my mama said but I needed to wait until Kayla was out of the car. I didn't want her to hear me and her aunt cutting up. She had already seen enough bullshit for one day. I hate I reacted the way I did. I didn't even think about Kayla being there. Seeing him put his hands on my sister triggered something inside of me.

After driving for almost forty minutes, I pulled up to Bernice's house in Jonesboro. Bryce had bought his mother a beautiful three-bedroom home with two and a half bathrooms. He was getting money because he worked for my brother, but he refused to get out of the hood. Tez has been telling him that he and my sister need to move, but he refuses.

Bryce and my sister love that ghetto shit. That's another reason why Jermaine is in his feelings about Tez not putting him on. He felt like since he looked out for Bryce he should have been willing to do the same for him. The difference is Bryce grew up in the hood and was already pushing dope before he met Tez. It was something that he was used to doing, he just needed Tez to elevate him to another level. Jermaine, on the other hand, was doing shit just to be doing it. We went inside and talked to Bernice for a few minutes before leaving out and heading to Cumberland Mall.

"So, let me tell you what Ma told me. She said we need to start respecting Dion because she loves him and he's moving in with her. Apparently, they're supposed to be getting married," I said during the drive.

"I know you fucking lying," Myra replied.

"Dead ass, I told her congratulations and okay. She won't have to worry about me going over there. I definitely need to look into a baby sitter for Kayla now."

"Shit, I hope she going to city hall to elope, because if she having a wedding she can save my invite," Myra said seriously.

I agreed with Myra one hundred percent there. I wasn't about to go to a wedding that I didn't approve of. Hopefully my mother came to her senses before it came to that point. We talked during the remainder of the drive to the mall.

While at the mall we were able to get everything that we needed, then we grabbed lunch and headed back to Myra's house. She needed to do my hair, so I was just about to hide out there until it was time for us to leave tonight. Jermaine had been blowing up my phone to the point where I had to silence it. I didn't feel like talking to him right now. I was going to enjoy my day and deal with him when I get home tonight.

CHAPTER FOUR
JERMAINE

When I woke up it was almost one o'clock. I got up and took a leak then looked around for Mercedes. She had left with Makayla and didn't even say anything. I knew that she was definitely in her feelings because she never does shit like this. If she leaves the house she lets me know first in order to see if I have something to do. I tried calling her ass again and she still didn't answer.

Tori had been blowing me up and I was trying to figure out why because I had just seen her this morning. I was trying to figure out why she wasn't passed out sleep the way I was earlier. Since Cedes wasn't here and not answering her phone, I decided to call Tori back.

"Hello, what took you so long to call me back?" she asked, confusing the hell out of me. This was some shit I wasn't used to. Mercedes doesn't even call questioning me like this unless she needed something important. Other than if I was outside, she pretty much let me be. That's how it was so easy for me to sneak around with Tori.

"Hey, did you forget that I left your house early this morning? I was tired as hell when I got home and passed out. I'm just now waking up not too long ago," I lied.

"Jermaine, it's almost three o'clock. I know you didn't sleep that long with a three-year-old in the house. Where your baby mama at?"

"Why you worried about where she at?" I asked.

This bitch was starting to act like the feds with this weird shit. I could already tell getting her pregnant was the worst thing I could have ever done. She never gave me crazy vibes before, but now she was acting like a couple of screws had popped loose.

"Because I'm trying to figure out if that's why you didn't answer me. You was probably laid up with her."

"My baby mama and my daughter were both gone when I got in this morning. I don't have time for this shit right now so I'll call you later," I told her, ready to hang up the phone.

"No wait, I'm sorry. I'm just stressed right now. Me and my parents got into an argument this morning because they heard us having sex. Now they're talking about if I can't keep you out of this house then I have to go. I told them that wasn't happening and that I'm pregnant. Now they're kicking me out and I only have a month to find somewhere to go."

"Well if all of that is going on maybe now isn't a good time to have a baby," I stated, hoping she'd take the hint and suggest getting rid of it.

"I already told you that I'm not getting an abortion. That just means we need to get up and start looking for a place of our own now. I was thinking you can pick me up tomorrow and we can go look."

"I can't, my baby mama has to work tomorrow so I have to be home to watch my daughter."

That part was the truth. Mercedes does have to work tomorrow from 10 to 6. When her father passed away, both of his businesses went to Montez since he was the oldest. He decided to make the construction company a family business. Myra and Mercedes ran the office there. I knew that they kept contracts, so I was starting to think Mercedes was actually making more money than what she is telling me.

"You can bring your daughter with you. I already went on Zillow and did apps and scheduled viewings. I'm off tomorrow so that's the only day I have available."

"Nah, I can't do that. My baby mama will trip if she finds out I had my daughter around another woman. My child is three years old and knows how to talk very clear."

"Now you're just making up excuses. We've been together for six months now. I should have met your daughter a long time ago. Our baby is about to be her sibling anyway. That means you still ain't told your baby mama about us like you were supposed to. She has to know that you were going to eventually move on. Maybe if we meet in person the transition of all of this will be easier. I mean, your daughter is going to have to be around me anyway because how else will you see her when we move in together?"

Tori's mouth was going a hundred miles a minute and everything she was saying was going in one ear and out the other. All the shit she was talking about was never going to happen. I'll give her some of the money from what I make tonight as a down payment on a house to rent, but that was about as much as I could do. I had fun with her but sometimes good things have to come to an end and this was going to be one. Once she was settled into a place I was going to call things off with her. I was just going to have to be a man and tell the truth.

"Right now just isn't a good time for me to be introducing y'all. I'm good with you finding a place for us though. Send me over what you found and I'll let you know what I like then we can take it from there. You can go view the places and if you like it I'll give you the down payment," I replied.

"I swear if I find out you're on some bullshit and still fucking your baby mama, it's going to be a problem," she warned me.

"I told you that you don't have anything to worry about. You are sitting up here tripping for nothing. Calm down, all of that stress can't be good for the baby," I told her.

I stayed on the phone with Tori for about twenty minutes before we hung up. She was acting like she didn't want to get off the phone. I had to lie and say it was my OG calling. Mercedes' ass still hadn't called me back yet and I needed her car to make that move tonight. If she don't pick up I'm going to have to get Rob to drive us. I still didn't know if Don was going with us or not.

I sat around the house waiting for Mercedes until almost seven. I decided to call her phone one more time.

"Hello," Mercedes asked, sounding irritated.

"Mercedes, where the fuck are you? I been calling your ass all day."

"I'm out with the girls making moves like you were last night," she replied sarcastically.

I swear if she was in front of me right now, I would have slapped the shit out of her smart-mouth ass and dealt with the consequences later.

"Stop fucking playing with me. I need you to come home so I can use the car to make a few runs tonight. If I can take care of this all of our money issues will be handled."

"I know you don't expect me to stop what I'm doing and come running home to you after the shit you pulled last night."

"Come on Cedes, this is important. I should have called and told you what was going on."

"I'm sorry, but I'm not coming home right now. I'm kid free

and spending the day with my siblings. I'm on my way to my brother's event right now and I'm not planning on leaving until I'm tired."

"So that's what we on now?" I asked, not believing how she was acting. These bitches was really playing with my top today.

"How is me wanting spend time with my family me being on anything? I don't say anything when you go see yours."

"I just told you that I need the car. You can come get me and I can drop you off and once I'm done, I'll come back and get you," I said, trying to reason with her.

"Nah, I'm good on that. I'll see you when I get home, if you decide to come back tonight," she said, hanging up on me.

I knew me not coming home last night was going to make her mad but I didn't think it would be this bad. I couldn't even get mad at her about what she was doing because I brought this on myself. I shot Rob a text and told him to come grab me. I needed to think of a new plan now anyway because I couldn't go shoot up a block that my girl was on.

I took a quick shower then got dressed in a pair of black joggers and a black t-shirt. Grabbing my wallet from the dresser, I put it inside of my pocket and got my house keys. By the time I walked in the living room Rob sent a text saying he was outside. I locked up the apartment and headed outside to the car.

"What's up man, thanks for coming to get me," I said once I was in the car.

"It's cool, where Mercedes at?"

"Man, I didn't get in until seven this morning and I didn't get a chance to shower before she saw me. We got into an argument and she waited until I fell asleep then left. She been gone all day and talking about she at the block party and ain't coming home until she's tired."

"Damn man, I told your ass to be careful. She gone end up kicking your ass out," he said, stating the obvious.

"I know, I'm going to have to stop fucking around on her. She don't deserve half the shit I'm doing to her."

"So what's the move for tonight? I know you not about to go shoot up the block with her out there."

"Nah, we got to come up with a new plan, but drive me over there first so I can talk to Cedes real quick."

"Aight, don't go over there starting no shit with that girl knowing her people out there," he warned me.

"I'm not. I just want to talk to her," I said.

Rob pulled off and we headed to the area where the party was. There were cars parked everywhere and people all in the road. Even if Mercedes wasn't here we was going to have to come up with a new plan. There was no way we would have been able to make it through here smoothly. The minute we tried to drive off we'd fall into a trap.

Rob ended up having to park damn near half a mile up the street. We got out of the car and took the walk up the road. I was looking around for Mercedes but it was going to be hard to spot her through this big ass crowd. I'm assuming since this her brother's shit she'll more than likely be in front of his trap close by him. Whenever she and Myra go out with him he keeps them close to him. The crazy part about this is I don't know which house is his trap house. Meech only told us the block but not the address. If a party wasn't going on it probably would've been easier to find.

"Yo, there go Cedes right there," Rob said, bumping my shoulder.

I looked in the direction that he was talking about. I had to do a double take because her hair was different than how it was when she left the house and she had on different clothes.

On top of that she was smiling in some nigga's face, causing me to pick up the pace of my walk.

I walked up to her and she acted like she didn't even see me at first.

"Mercedes, what the fuck are you doing?" I asked.

"I'm hanging out like I told you I was. What are you doing here?"

"I was coming to see if we could talk. I wanted to make things right with us but I guess being a hoe was more important."

"Jermaine, fuck you. How dare you call me a hoe when all the fuck your ass do is lie. I'm so tired of your shit."

"What the fuck are you talking about? I told you what happened last night."

"Yeah, and what you told me was a lie. Every time I ask you something all you do is fucking lie. You're a lying liar," she yelled, getting the attention of some of the partygoers.

Although she was being loud and causing a scene, she was looking good as hell. The long sew-in she had in her hair had deep waves and she had on a red halter top and short blue jean shorts with a pair of red and black Air Max. She had on a silver chain with a pair of silver earrings and a bracelet. She was out here getting these niggas attention rightfully.

When I met Mercedes she was two hundred seventy-five pounds, but that didn't take away from her beauty. She had a smooth caramel complexion with light-brown, almond-shaped eyes, deep dimples, and long black hair. She was self-conscious about her weight but I taught her how to be confident in herself. My guys thought I was tripping by dating a big girl but I didn't pay them any attention.

Mercedes was laid back with a bomb ass personality. We were able to vibe and nothing else mattered. Not to mention she gave me her virginity and I ended up falling in love with that pussy. I loved the shit so much that I put a baby in her ass. I wanted to make sure that she never went anywhere. I guess the joke was on me though, because when our daughter turned one Cedes started eating right and hitting the gym. She lost one hundred pounds in a year now her body is toned and looking good. She got thick thighs and a fat ass with big breasts. The only thing she missing is a flat stomach, but it's flat enough for her to wear whatever she wants.

Had this been a year ago I wouldn't even be having these problems with her. She wasn't even going outside like this before she lost weight. Now every time Myra or one of her girls suggest that they go out, her ass getting dressed ready to follow behind them. I don't think she'd cheat on me but from walking up on her right now, she was definitely entertaining the niggas.

"You're causing a scene," I told her, gently grabbing her arm so we could get away from the crowd.

"Jermaine, let me go. I don't want to hear shit you talking about. The time for us to talk was this morning but instead, your ass showered and went to bed like shit didn't happen."

"Jermaine, let my sister's arm go. She don't have to talk to your ass if she don't want to. You coming out here fucking up her vibe," Myra stated.

On everything I love, I wish Myra was a nigga for one day so I could beat her ass. I hated her just as much as she hated me. She was always in me and Cedes business. It's been like this since day one. The way she be acting half the time you'd think she wanted the dick. I wouldn't even hook up any of my guys with that bitch. Don't get me wrong now, she's fine as fuck. Her and Mercedes look just alike. She's about fifteen pounds lighter than Mercedes but her ass and titties is bigger since she got her body done courtesy of her baby daddy.

"Myra, mind your own damn business. I'm not about to kidnap her ass. I just want to talk to her."

"Aye, don't talk to my sister like that," Mercedes replied.

At this point I could tell we weren't going to get anywhere. Mercedes had obviously been drinking and smoking. This was yet another thing that changed about her since we started dating. Well, I guess she couldn't do much of anything at first since she was only seventeen. Once she started hitting the streets she started picking up all kinds of habits. It was like all the hard work I put into molding her to be the kind of woman I wanted didn't matter anymore. I felt like I had wasted my motherfucking time for the past four years.

I was about to respond to Mercedes when Tez came walking our way. I already knew it wasn't going to be any hope for me now.

"What's up? Is everything good over here?" Tez asked, looking between me and Mercedes.

"Yeah, we good, I just wanted to talk to your sister for a minute."

"You can talk to her without touching her," he told me, looking down at my hand on her arm.

I removed my hand and took a step back, letting him know that I didn't want any problems. It was like I could feel his guys watching me and waiting for me to make the wrong move. I wasn't on that with them though. I just wanted to keep the peace and talk to my girl.

"Mercedes, can we please go talk?"

"When you called me earlier I told you that I didn't want to talk to you. I told you that we could discuss the shit when I get home. Clearly this isn't home and nothing has changed."

"Alright Cedes, I'll see you when you get home," I said, walking away.

I didn't have time to continue going back and forth with

her. I still needed to go to the trap and figure out how to handle this shit for Meech. After what just happened tonight, I needed that money more than anything because my ass could end up homeless any day now.

"You good, bro?" Rob asked as we walked back to his car.

"Yeah, I'm good. Let's head to the spot so we can get this over with."

We wasn't pushing major weight or anything so we didn't call the place that we hung out at a trap house. It was just somewhere that we hung out at to chill and bring bitches from time to time. I'm hoping once all this shit is done and we put our money together we can make it our trap house. It's in a decent area and in a lowkey spot. My goal is to move enough weight until I get to the point where I don't even have to touch the shit.

When we made it to the car, Rob started it and pulled off. He looked like he wanted to say something but instead, he stayed quiet. I was thankful for that because I didn't feel like talking right now. I had a lot going on in my mind at one time. I was about to do my first hit and I didn't even have a clear mind. Mercedes picked the wrong time to start showing her ass.

They always say a man can't take a woman doing dirt. They ain't never lied about that shit. I'm sitting here with my chest hurting, feeling like it's the end of the world. If I wasn't in the car with Rob, my ass would probably be crying. It didn't matter that I had a baby on the way by another woman. All of that seemed far less worse than finding out the woman you love is falling out of love with you. Shit, at this point it wouldn't surprise me if she finds another nigga and let him hit since she thinks I'm cheating.

This isn't the first time that Mercedes has caught me cheating. She found out I was fucking around on her when she was pregnant. She gave me the silent treatment for a couple of weeks but eventually she forgave me. I was hoping that would be the case this time but I could tell it wasn't. I went low and she went to hell. It's funny how all it takes is for a woman to lose weight for her entire personality to change. I guess it's because once the weight is gone the confidence is built.

When we pulled up to our hangout spot we saw Don's car parked out front. Don was sitting down talking to one of the young niggas. He looked up at us and nodded his head. I'm assuming since he's here it means he's down for the job, which was a good thing since we needed to come up with a new plan.

"What took y'all so long? I thought we was meeting three hours ago," Don said.

"Yeah, it was a change of plans. Some shit came up and I didn't know if you were in so I didn't reach out," I answered.

"Everything good now? Are we going to do what it takes to get the money?" Don countered.

"Yeah, we're still going to do it, but it's going to be after the block party dies down. Right now it's too many innocent people out there. It's kids playing around plus women everywhere. Not to mention all the cars out there. If we acted now we would pretty much be putting ourselves in a trap that we can't get out of," I explained.

"Okay, what's the plan then?" Ron asked.

"We go over there and wait it out in the cut. Once it seems like everybody is gone then we'll make our move."

We hung out at the spot for a couple hours just chilling and smoking before we felt like it was a good time to leave. The four of us climbed inside the black Escalade and headed to Tez's trap. The block was a lot calmer now but there was still a few people out there. I didn't see Tez or Mercedes outside so that meant they were most likely gone already, which was even better. I don't understand why Meech didn't want to just take

Tez out and get it over with. I guess that's rich nigga business and above my pay grade.

"Don, you and AL will take the back while me and Rob take the front. The main objective is to take Josh out. That's what will get us paid," I reminded them.

We waited around for about an hour until the coast was clear. We all put on our ski masks and parked the truck out front so we could run in and right back out. I wasn't thinking about getting somebody else to be a driver. We was already giving AL fifteen thousand. I didn't want to split any more of my money.

AL and Don ran around back while me and Rob took the front. I turned the doorknob and the door was locked, so I kicked it in. People instantly started shooting and I just started shooting back. This wasn't the first time I used a gun because I've practiced at the range, but this was the first time I was shooting people. I didn't anticipate these many people being here at night.

"Take what you want!" a nigga said with his hands up.

"Where the fuck does Tez lay his head?" I asked while Ron and AL filled a bag with money and drugs.

"I don't know where Tez ass live. You wasting your time if that's what you here for. You might as well kill us all now," he replied.

I could see it in his eyes that he was telling the truth. I already knew he most likely didn't know where Tez lived. Anybody that worked out of Tez's trap were considered bottom feeders. Half the niggas that worked for him probably never got a chance to even meet him. This is only one of many traps that he has.

"Where that nigga Josh at?" I questioned.

"I don't know. When he leaves he doesn't give us updates."

"Get him on the phone now. Meech got some words for

him. It's either you or him," I threatened, aiming the gun at his head.

"Well you might as well shoot because I'm not setting Josh up for you. I'm just as good as dead either way," the guy responded.

I had to give it to Tez and Josh. They had some loyal niggas on their team. I only hoped to get some niggas on my team like them. Too bad loyalty only got you so far. Lifting my gun, I shot the nigga in both of his legs. Adrenaline surged through my body from the feeling of pulling the trigger.

"Call Josh now!" I bellowed.

"Fuck you nigga. You call him," the guy spat. I let off another round in his shoulder and he didn't even flinch.

I raised my gun to let off another shot when out of nowhere, I heard gunfire. Looking behind me, I noticed AL, Rob, and Don laid out on the floor. Taking a step over to see what was going on, I noticed Josh and a couple more niggas. I started shooting their way as I grabbed the duffle bag from the table that Don had filled with money and drugs, then made a beeline for the back door.

Josh chased me but he couldn't catch up with me. All I knew was bullets was flying everywhere and I was hauling ass. I needed to get as far away from there as possible or my ass was going to be laid out as well. I ran for I don't know how long until I ordered an Uber to my mama's house. I needed a minute to catch my breath and try to figure all of this out. I didn't kill Josh so the money I was going to get from Meech is down the drain. However, the money and shit that's in this bag will make up for it.

It's fucked up what happened to Rob, Don, and AL. I'm just hoping Josh gets rid of their bodies and not figure out that I'm connected to them. If that connection is made then it's over for me. It won't matter that I didn't pull the trigger on Josh. My entire family will be in jeopardy behind my bullshit.

Halfway during the ride to my mama's house, I felt a sharp pain in the back of my leg. I lifted my pants leg and felt something wet and sticky. I had got shot and never even realized it. I'm glad I did decide to go to my mama's house instead of home first because there was no way I could explain to Mercedes how I got shot. She would automatically put two and two together once she hears about what went down tonight. Luckily the drive to my mama's house was only ten minutes.

When we pulled up to my mom's house it was pitch black. I didn't expect anything different since it was almost two in the morning. Grabbing the duffle bag, I got out of the Uber and took the keys to my mom's house out of my pocket and used them to enter her house. I dropped the bag on the floor then limped in the dark and made my way to the bathroom then turned on the light.

Lifting my pants leg up, I did my best to try and see the wound but I couldn't because it was on the back of my leg and I couldn't get a good angle in the mirror. I didn't want to wake my mother up because she would ask too many questions and I would have no choice but to tell her the truth because she can tell when I'm lying. Instead, I limped down the hall to my sister's room. I knocked on the door and waited for about a minute and she didn't answer, so I knocked again.

"What Ma," Kelly yelled.

"It's not Mama. It's me," I answered.

I heard her saying something but I couldn't make out what it was. She was probably talking shit for me waking her up.

"Jermaine, what do you want? Did Mercedes finally come to her senses and leave your ass?" Kelly asked.

All I could do was shake my head because Kelly was always talking about Cedes leaving me. When Mercedes was living with us she and Kelly got close. Cedes was the like the sister Kelly never had. She acted like she loved Cedes more than me. She even threatened to tell Mercedes the shit I was doing behind her back. I had to remind her that she was my blood sister. That didn't mean shit to her just like it didn't to my mother. My mother told me a long time ago that I better not do no dirt in front of her because she was telling. She was a woman first before anything.

"I need you to check my leg out for me," I told her.

"Nigga, you woke me up in the middle of the night to see something on your leg?" she asked with an attitude.

"Just come in the bathroom and look at it," I told her, walking away.

I went in the bathroom and lifted my pants leg back up while I waited on her. It was taking her so long I thought she wasn't going to come for real, then she finally walked in the bathroom.

"Oh my god Maine, there's a hole in your leg. How did you get shot?"

"I was in the wrong place at the wrong time. Do you think you can get the bullet out?"

"Dude, I'm a medical assistant. Not a damn doctor," she said.

"I know, all you have to do is get a blade and tweezers from the first-aid kit and see if you see a bullet then stitch me up. I know you know how to do stitches."

"Man, I swear you a dumb ass nigga. You outside doing some shit you don't have any business doing. I told you to stop doing that fake gangsta shit."

"Shut up, you don't know what you talking about it."

"Boy, I'm not crazy. If this was an accident your dumb ass would've went to the hospital. You better not be in no shit that will bring problems this way," she warned me.

Kelly was only two years older than me but the way she acted you would think she raised me or some shit. She was always chastising me and trying to keep me on track, but the nine to five life just wasn't for me. She always said I was too smart for the shit I was doing and maybe I was, but I didn't see any other way to get the kind of money I needed fast.

"Can you just mind your business and keep it down before you wake Mama?" I asked.

"Boy, Mama is knocked out, and don't tell me to mind my business when you came waking me up. You lucky I love you or I'd allow you to bleed to death," she said.

I sat on the toilet seat while Kelly grabbed the peroxide and the first-aid kit. She immediately started working on my leg. It hurt like hell since she didn't have anything to numb it for me. When it came down to the stitching I had to bite down on a rag. It felt like I was about to pass the fuck out. Once she finished stitching she wrapped a bandage around my leg. As long as I kept it wrapped up I could hide that it was a gun wound from Mercedes.

"Thanks Kelly," I told her once she was done.

"You're welcome. You need to leave whatever you're doing in the streets alone before next time you'll need more than your leg stitched up."

"I hear you." I popped a couple pain pills then limped back to the living room. I grabbed the duffle bag from by the door and sat on the couch. Once I heard Kelly's door close I sat down on the couch. I understood where she was coming from. She only wanted the best for me, but what she didn't know was that I was just getting started.

I opened the duffle bag and started counting the money. By the time I finished it was at fifty thousand dollars. It was definitely more than what Meech was offering for killing Josh so the way I look at it, I came out on top either way.

It was almost four in the morning and I was already going to get accused of being with a woman, so there was no need to rush home. I was just going to sleep here and then call Mercedes with my mother around before heading home. Mercedes already know my mother or sister won't cover for me if I was out on bullshit.

CHAPTER FIVE
MARTEZ

A couple days ago Meech made a move on me. He stole fifty thousand dollars and a kilo of coke from me, so it's only right that I hit his warehouse. He should know by now that I'm not to be fucked with.

The beef that I have with him isn't even my beef. This is some shit that stemmed back from when my pops was in the game. They was rivals and so this old nigga decided to pick up the shit with me. He hated that a young nigga came into the game and caught up to his level. I tried having a sit down with him so that we could come to a common ground, but he didn't want to do that. He has literally been my only problem throughout the years. The only reason I haven't put a bullet in his head yet is because he's my uncle. Him and my mother have the same father but different mothers.

Up until now it had been non-violent situations with us. He'd have one of my traps robbed and I'd set one of his on fire. He knows I don't half do anything. I don't like that kind of attention. I had to fucking get rid of those bodies and pay off a couple police not to report the shooting.

I was on my way to the crib to chill with my woman when I got the call from Josh about what happened. I just knew he had to be bullshitting with me because it had been a while since me and Meech exchanged words. I don't even know what the hell would possess him to come at me right now. I ain't been on his turf and as far as I know, he hadn't been on mine. I tried calling his ass afterward and he didn't answer. I told my mama what happened and she tried reaching him and he ain't answer her either. The only option he left me with was to retaliate. I don't see no other way.

I gotta keep the family fed (yeah, yeah)
Look, just talked to pops about the feds
I ain't gon' lie, he had me scared, uh
I feel 'em coming, nigga (yeah)
I'll keep on running, nigga (yeah)
If we go down bad, keep it a hundred, nigga
My girl all in my ear screaming, "spend some time"
I promise I'll be here when I can get some time
Right now, I got to get what's mine (for sure)
I'll be thuggin' 'til the end of time
And fuck these niggas 'cause they lame
Since they love saying my name
Make sure you write the truest in the motherfuckin' game
On my tombstone when they bury me
By the river, they will carry me
Finally, I'll be resting in peace
Finally, finally

I listened to "Tombstone" by Rod Wave as I drove around Atlanta. This was something I did to clear my head before I had major decisions to make. I always listened to this and "Green Light" by Rod Wave. The lyrics to that song spoke volumes to me because it reminded me of my life. This was a life that was never meant for me. My father worked hard as hell to make sure me and my brother Stephen didn't end up following in his footsteps.

Stephen didn't give a fuck what my father was talking about. He wanted to be just like him. He wanted the money, bitches, houses, and luxury cars. He dropped out of high school his junior year and started selling dope. At first, him and my father butt heads about the situation, then my father decided to teach him the right way because he didn't want him to end up dead or in jail.

I, on the other hand, was a different story. I went to school and got great grades. I graduated from high school at the top of my class and went to University of Georgia.

I was working toward my bachelor's degree in criminal justice. The plan after that was to get my law degree at Georgia State University.

Growing up, my pops used to always say as much as I liked to debate shit and prove that I was right, I needed to be a lawyer. I agreed with him, which is why I went to college. That school shit came natural to me. By the end of my junior year I had a 3.8 GPA and my teachers used to always talk about how bright of a future I was going to have. It was like they was surprised at how smart I was since I grew up in the hood. I pushed myself to keep my grades up because I didn't want to be a statistic. I wanted to make my family proud of me. More importantly, I wanted my pops proud of me. I wanted him to know how his hard work had paid off.

My father passed away two weeks before it was time for me to start my senior year of college. Before that I was excited to get back to school and finish up my last year. I hand landed an internship at the Juvenile Center and I was going to work there while attending law school. My entire fucking life was literally planned out for me and all it took was one day for everything I worked so hard for to change.

When my father died, that triggered something inside of me. I lost focus and without that I no longer had the same hopes and dreams. You would think after he died I would have pushed even harder to get my degree so that I could find his killer and get justice. Nope, that wasn't the case.

It was like something snapped inside of me and my entire life and personality changed. I no longer gave a fuck about who was proud of me. All I could think about was avenging my father's death because he didn't deserve that shit.

I started hanging out with Stephen more. Even though he was younger than me he knew more about the game. We were a force to reckon with when we were together. I got my weight up and eventually we got the nigga who killed my father. That was the first of many bodies I dropped. It was like killing them niggas woke up something that I had submerged.

I'm a perfectionist and I love chess. Everything I touch turns into gold because I think before I react. That's one of the reasons why I'm still out in the streets and never been locked up before. Even though Stephen was in the game longer than me he didn't move smart, and that's how he ended up in the predicament that he's in.

I guess jail is better than being dead. Nah, fuck that shit. I'd rather they bury me than I end up in jail doing football numbers. I couldn't imagine having someone tell me when I could eat, sleep, and shit every day. Not to mention, who would look out for my sisters if I was in jail?

I loved my sisters more than life itself. Those are the only people I would lay my life on the line for because they've always been innocent in this. I wish I had a better relationship with Kiana. That's something I'm working on now, but I look out for her. I have people that keep an eye on all three of my sisters around the clock. That's the price to pay to be the boss.

I don't plan on doing this shit forever. I'm not with all that fancy shit. I'm working on building a foundation for my family. I want it where no one in my family will ever have to touch drugs in their life to get by. I don't want them to have to struggle and endure the shit I went through the past eight years. I did all this shit for the sake of my family. I bear the cross so they don't have to.

Within the next couple of years, I'm going to propose to my girl and start a family if she's still around. It takes a strong motherfucker to deal with me. I'm not one of those niggas in the streets that can't control their dick. I'm as loyal as it comes to a street nigga. I'm not going to say I ain't never slipped up and cheated on somebody before, but it's not something that happens often.

I'm financially stable to take care of kids right now but I have too much bullshit going on in the streets. I already gotta worry about if a nigga gone try to do something to one of my sisters to get back at me. I can't worry about them doing something to my seed as well. Right now I'm the dependable big brother and uncle.

I don't have the time that it requires to take care of a baby either. I'm in the streets more than I'm home. On any given day I'm hitting the pavement sixteen hours out of twenty-four. My other eight hours are spent trying to get some sleep and making sure my family is straight.

The sound of my phone ringing pulled me away from my thoughts. I looked down at the screen and saw that it was Kaye.

"Hey baby," I answered.

"Hey, are you still coming over tonight?" she asked.

"That's the plan. It all depends on how everything turns out tonight," I replied.

"Come on Tez, that's what you said the other day. Do you realize we haven't seen each other or had sex in over a week?"

I had been so busy putting the plan together for tonight that I lost track of the days. Sex had been the last thing on my mind but at the same time, I didn't mean to neglect my girl behind this street shit. This was another reason why we've been together for almost two years and don't live together. I have to be able to make moves without nobody keeping track of me. I'm not saying Kaye is a snake and that I can't trust her. I'm just saying she not built for this life and if somebody put a gun to her head, she'd sing like a canary.

"My bad baby, I've been busy. You know I have a lot of shit going on right now. I gave you the option to take a step away from this relationship until I can give you the time that you need. The offer still stands and I won't have any hard feelings," I assured her.

"Tez, like I told you last time, I don't want that option. All I'm saying is that I miss you and want to spend time with you. That doesn't mean I don't understand what you have going on in the streets. What the fuck I look like investing two years into a relationship only to step back and allow another bitch to step in and take my place?"

"It's not about anybody taking your place, Kaye. It's about you being able to have peace of mind and not worry about what I have going on."

"Is it another woman or something? I'm a big girl. I can handle it."

I sighed because this conversation was the last thing I needed to be having right now. The purpose of my drive was so I can focus and clear my head. I can't go in ready to knock a nigga's skull back with thoughts of my relationship on my mind.

"I can't do this right now. I'll come over once I'm done handling business but I can't give you an exact time."

"Okay, see you tonight," she said, hanging up the phone.

I shook my head as I continued my job. That was all her ass wanted me to say anyway. She knew what buttons to push to get her way. I love her so I allow her to get away with the shit. She's been there for me whenever I needed her since day one.

When I met Kaye she was working at the strip club to pay her way through college. She was too beautiful and smart to be taking her clothes off for a living. I offered her a job at our construction company and she took it. She wasn't making as much money as she was from stripping but it was enough to pay for school. I pretty much made up the rest with what I was giving her. She'd proven her loyalty to me on more than one occasion.

I just needed to make time to toughen her ass up like I did Myra and Mercedes. I took them both to the range and taught them how to shoot. They also attended self-defense classes. Even though I have men watching them, they watch from a distance, so anything could happen. They have their conceal to carry license and all. I made sure they handled shit the legal way.

After driving around for about another hour, I headed to my warehouse so I could talk to my men and come up with a game plan. I wasn't allowing another day to go by without knowing how I was going to handle this shit with Meech. He was playing checkers while I was playing chess. I was going to let everything die down and hit him when he least expected it, and when I hit, I hit hard.

CHAPTER SIX
MERCEDES

For the past couple of weeks Jermaine has been acting weird and I don't know what the hell is going on with him. He's been coming and going out of the house at all kinds of hours, and then yesterday he pulled up to the house in a black Charger. I don't know where the car came from or where he even got the money from. When I asked him all he said was that he's been out hustling. I knew that shit was shady because he been hustling for almost a year and ain't made that kind of money before.

I took a long hot shower and went back in my bedroom where Jermaine was sitting on the edge of the bed looking crazy.

"So you're really going out tonight without me?" he asked.

"Yes, I am. Bryce's mother is watching Makayla so I don't have a reason not to go," I replied.

Tonight is Bryce's birthday and he's having a party at Sanctuary Nightclub. Jermaine was supposed to go with me and then all of a sudden, he's busy and can't go. I guess he thought that was going to stop me from going, but he thought wrong.

"What time are you coming back?" he asked.

"I don't know, it's a club, Maine. I don't ask you these questions when you go out so why are you doing it with me?"

"It's different from when I go because you're a woman. I know how to take care of myself and nobody will try anything with me."

"Ain't nobody gone try anything with me. It's not like I'm going to the club alone. My sister, brother, and their friends will be there, so I'm pretty sure nobody will start anything with me. Also, I know how to take care of myself."

"I know you can Cedes, I was just saying," he responded.

I grabbed my clothes off of the bed and got dressed in a pair of black shorts that went a couple inches past my ass and a black sleeveless shirt that tied around my neck. I put a silver belt through the hoops of my shorts to bring more to my outfit. I finished the look with a pair of silver gladiator sandal heels.

I put my hair in a half up-half down style, and my makeup was done naturally because I didn't need it and I rarely wear it unless I'm going out. I put on my diamond necklace, earrings, and bracelet that I got for my birthday from Myra and Bryce.

"What do you—who you texting?" I interrupted my own question because he was sitting down smiling at his phone.

His smile immediately dropped after hearing my voice.

"I wasn't texting anybody," he replied. "Just because I'm smiling doesn't mean that I'm texting anybody. I could have been watching something funny."

"Are you serious right now? That's really the best you could come up with? There was no sound coming from your phone and your ass was smiling not laughing."

"Don't start that insecure shit now, Cedes. You're the one that's about to go out looking like a hoe."

"Jermaine, you got me fucked up. You better get out of my face before I knock your ass upside your head," I warned him.

Jermaine got up and left the room, slamming the door behind him. I don't know what's going on with him but I'm going to find out. It's at the point where I'm about to tell his ass that I'm moving and he needs to find his own place. My patience is running thin as hell and I'm ready to do me.

One thing I can't stand is a liar. Especially one that thinks I'm stupid. I was mad at the fact that he lied about texting. That alone meant he was texting a bitch. I saw his damn fingers moving. Then the nigga had the nerve to call me insecure. I might have been insecure back then, but that shit is dead now. I'm confident in everything I do.

I stood in front of the full-length mirror and admired myself. My body wasn't perfect but I worked hard as hell to get it to the point where it's at now and I love it. I won't allow Jermaine or anybody else to make me feel different.

I grabbed my purse and left out of the room. Jermaine was sitting on the couch looking stupid with his dumb ass. I grabbed my keys and was about to walk out of the house when he stopped me.

"So you about to leave without saying anything?" he asked.

"What do you want me to say? You saw me getting dressed so that meant I was about to go."

"You're driving yourself there?"

"No, I'm leaving my car at Myra's house and riding with her."

"Why are you doing all of that? I can drop you off and pick you up if you want me too," he offered.

"Nah, I'm good. I'll see you later," I told him before walking out.

I wasn't about to allow him to dictate when I move. I'm trying to figure out how his ass too busy to go out with me but at the same time not busy enough to drop me off and pick me up.

Getting in my car, I drove to Myra's house. When I got there she was already standing out front with Bryce and his sister Qiana. I spoke and hugged everybody. Qiana's ass held me tighter. She was always doing that shit. She's bisexual and be begging to taste me and I tell her ass no every time.

We got in Myra's BMW since she was the designated driver. The club was only twenty minutes away so the car ride was quick. She parked in front and gave her keys to the valet driver. The line was wrapped around the wall but Bryce knew the club owner so we didn't have to wait in line. He spoke to the security guard and we entered. When we got to the VIP section it was already people in there. I spoke then sat down next to Myra and Qiana.

We started taking shots and listening to the music. I loved the atmosphere and vibe that was going on. I was about to take my third shot when this fine ass brother came walking in the VIP area. I had to do a double take at how good this man looked.

He had a Hershey's complexion standing at about 6'2 with a low cut and waves that would make a bitch sea sick. His smile glistened in the club lights as his dimples damn near made me melt. He wore a short-sleeve, white, fitted Versace shirt that showed off his biceps, with a pair of black Amiri jeans. For shoes he wore a pair of white Versace high-top sneakers. He had a silver cross chain around his neck with a diamond AP watch on his wrist.

He looked around the room and his piercing brown eyes met mine. It felt like he was peering into my soul, daring me to look away.

It wasn't until Bryce tapped him on the shoulder did he

look away. He gave him a brotherly hug and they exchanged a few words before walking our way.

"Rio, you already know my sister Qiana and my girl Myra. This other lovely lady is my sister Mercedes. She's actually Myra's lil' sister so that makes her family," Bryce said.

"What's up y'all," he said to Qiana and Mercedes before turning his attention to me.

"Hello beautiful, it's nice to meet you," he stated, extending his hand.

Usually I don't shake niggas' hands because half they ass don't wash their hands when they piss. However, he looked clean as hell so I extended my hand. His plump lips grazed my hand, causing me to squeeze my thighs together.

Everything about this man demanded respect without even asking for it. I flirted with niggas from time to time but none of them had me ready to step out on my relationship. This nigga had me ready to risk it all and all he said was hello. I had the same feeling in the pit of my stomach that I had when I met Jermaine. This was only the second time I've had butterflies in my stomach from a man. I had to tell my hormones to calm the fuck down.

"Bitch, speak back," Myra mumbled as she bumped my shoulder.

"Hey, it's nice to meet you as well," I finally said with a slight smile.

"Yo Rio, move around. This my girl," Qiana said, causing Myra to laugh.

I didn't find shit funny. Qiana know I hate when she do this shit and she does it every time when we're out.

"Oh, my bad lil' sis," he said, taking a step back.

I was about to respond when Qiana spoke back up.

"I'm just fucking with you. I wish she was mine but you're more her type than mine," she replied.

Qiana was a beautiful light-skinned female. She had thick thighs, a big ass, and perky breasts. If I ever decided to slide the other way, I would definitely do it with her. Unfortunately, right now I'm with team D. Not to mention I'm in a relationship.

"Okay, that's even better for me." He smirked, causing me to blush.

Bryce and Rio walked away to greet some of the other partygoers. Suddenly, my hand was feeling empty without Rio's hand in it. I had to remind myself how shit turned out with Jermaine after falling for him so quick.

"Girl, I know you gone get his number before you go," Myra asked so that I was the only one to hear her.

"I can't, you know I'm with Jermaine."

"Girl, don't mention that lame ass nigga's name. I know you not about to pass up the opportunity to get to know Rio."

"All he did was speak. That doesn't mean he likes me. He could've just been nice."

"Bitch, the way he was looking at you, he wanted to be more than nice. He was looking at you like you like you were the only bitch in here," Myra said.

I was about to respond when Tez and Josh came walking in. They spoke to Bryce and Rio before walking over to where we sat. Both Myra and I stood up to hug Tez. After hugging Tez, I leaned in to hug Josh.

"When you gone stop playing and give me a chance?" he whispered in my ear.

"You know I can't for a number of reasons. We already discussed this," I reminded him, taking a step back.

Josh had been trying to get with me for the past few months after I turned twenty-one. He knows that I'm in a relationship, and he's my brother's best friend. That reason alone would make shit awkward as hell. My brother needed people to look out for him and I wasn't about to get in between them. If something went wrong I already know Tez would choose my side.

I was about to sit back down when Rio motioned for me to come over where he was.

"I'll be right back," I said, walking away not waiting for a response.

Rio's hands gripped my waist as he pulled me close to his chest, causing the hairs on the back of my neck to stand up.

"You wanna dance with me?" he asked, bending down some so I could hear him.

I answered with my body and not my words. I slowly started rolling my hips against him as his hand started roaming my thighs. Allowing my body to relax against his, I kept up with the beat and danced like it was only me and him in the room. I could feel his member up against my pants and I could tell that he was packing. This is the reason why I'm always turning men's dances down. This is the first time I've ever felt this comfortable with a man other than Jermaine. I don't know what it is about him. It's too bad that I have a man so I was never going to get the chance to find out.

Once the song was over I attempted to walk away, but he pulled me right back on him. I stayed dancing with him for three more songs before he finally let me walk away. I went and sat back down next to Myra and she had a big ass grin on her face while Tez's ass was mugging me.

"How you know that nigga?" Tez asked.

"I don't know him. Bryce just introduced us," I replied.

"The way he was all over you it seemed like he knew you well. Do I need to do a background check on him?" Tez asked seriously.

"No Montez , it was just a dance. I doubt I'll ever see him again after tonight," I admitted.

"Yeah aight, just because you're twenty-one don't mean you're grown now," he said.

"Technically it do," I laughed.

"Tez, leave her alone. She's just having a little fun. Rio damn sure a better choice than Jermaine," Myra added.

"Aye, I don't need everybody in my business. We can talk about this later," I said, trying to thin the ice that was building.

Montez and Myra was always having a debate about what I should and shouldn't do. I love my siblings to death but it was like I had two mothers and two fathers.

"Oh, we definitely going to talk about this later," Montez pouted, causing me to laugh again.

After that small hiccup, we got back to drinking and dancing a bit. "Pussy Talk" by City Girls came on and all the bitches was up out of their seats, on the dance floor shaking they ass.

Boy, this pussy talk English, Spanish, and French (hello)

Boy, this pussy talk Euros, Dollars, and Yens (oww)

Boy, this pussy talk Bentleys, Rovers, and Benz

Boy, this pussy fly private to islands, to M's

Boy, this pussy talk Birkin, Gucci, Chanel (oww)

Boy, this pussy talk Louis, Pucci, YSL (YSL)

Boy, this pussy make movies, wetter than a whale (hahaha)

Boy, this pussy be choosing, draft, NFL (ching-ching)

I was up out of my seat, singing and dancing right along with it. At this point the liquor had kicked in and I was dancing with Qiana. Her lil' freaky ass was friskier than Rio was. I had to be careful before her ass tried turning me out for real.

I've never been with a woman before, but I can't lie and say I'm not curious about how it is. I've heard that a woman knows how to eat pussy better than a man. I just can't picture having sex with a woman one on one. I mean, if it was a threesome then it would probably be a different story. That's also on my list of things to do. I just haven't done one with Jermaine because he hasn't done shit to earn one. Knowing his sneaky ass, I'd give him a threesome and he'd start fucking with the girl behind my back.

By the time the song was over I was tired and needed to use the bathroom. I drank half a bottle of Voss water and grabbed Myra's hand so she could go with me.

"Where y'all going?" Tez asked.

"To the bathroom," I replied, pulling Myra along with me.

As we were walking out of the VIP area, Rio pulled me close by the waist.

"Come talk to me for a minute when you get back."

"Okay," I said, walking away.

"Now girl, what you gone do when he ask you for your number?"

"I'm going to tell him I got a man. I'm not about to lie."

"Bitch, does he look like he's the type of man that care about you telling him you got a man? He look like Mr. Steal Your Girl. Just so you know, if you don't give him your number, I will," Myra stated.

"Girl, don't give him my number. I'm not about to start something with somebody else while I got something already going on. I don't care what Jermaine is doing, I refuse to stoop to his level."

"Alright, I hear you."

There was a long ass line to the bathroom but luckily, it was moving fast. If I had to wait any longer than the five minutes it took, I was going to piss on myself. I used the bathroom then fixed my lipstick. Once we were done we went back to the area.

Myra went back to her seat and I stood next to Rio so we could talk.

"I don't beat around the bush so I'm just going to say it. I think you fine as fuck and you should get my number so I can get to know you better. I'm not on no just trying to fuck you or I wouldn't have asked for your number. I would have just been like let's get out of here."

"Wait, let me stop you there. I'm sorry if I gave you the wrong impression, but I'm not available. I'm in a relationship with my daughter's father."

"No offense sweetheart, and I mean this in the most humble way possible, fuck that nigga. The way you were dancing on me, you might be in a relationship but it ain't a happy and committed one. You don't have to give me your number right now but when the time comes, you'll give it to me. That relationship ain't about to last," he told me.

I was at a loss for words after what he just told me, so all I said was okay. With the way I've been feeling lately, he was absolutely right. I just didn't want to throw away a four-year relationship for Rio. That man looked like he had pussy thrown to him for breakfast, lunch, and dinner. I didn't want to just be another notch in his belt. I guess at this point, only time will tell.

CHAPTER SEVEN
JERMAINE

My life has been crazy since the day I robbed Tez's trap. I hired a few young niggas to come and work with me. I sold the kilo I stole and made thirty-five thousand off of that. Then I did a reup and broke that down for distribution. I gave Tori $3200 for the three-bedroom house she's renting in Jonesboro. Then another $15,000 to furnish the house. I told her to get whatever she wanted and that's exactly what she did.

I spent another $10,000 on the Charger I bought. It's not what I really wanted but it'll do for now. It was better than sharing a car with Mercedes. She had been acting like she ain't want to give me the car. She always seemed like she had something to do lately. I made sure to save $25,000 from the money that was stolen and the rest has been going toward building my foundation.

Next week I'm going to buy some stuff for Makayla even though she doesn't really need it. I feel bad not doing nothing for Mercedes and Makayla but I have to do it big for them. I want to be able to take them on a family vacation.

Today I was supposed to go to the club with Mercedes but I couldn't. I was trying my best to stay low because I had been receiving threats from Meech. The day after the hit went wrong, I called my cousin and told him to tell Meech I tried to handle Josh but all three of my people got killed. Told him thanks for the opportunity but I can't do this.

It was radio silence for about a week when Meech called me himself talking about I owe him $50,000 and a kilo of coke. Some kind of way he found out what I had stolen. At first I couldn't figure out how he knew since the only people that knew about what went down was dead.

A couple days later, I figured out how he found out. I had mentioned his name to the nigga that I shot. He must've told Josh and Josh told Tez. I'm guessing Tez confronted Meech about the shit and it all came back on me. I don't have the dope or the money to give him so I've been trying to hustle to get the rest of the money, but I'm nowhere near how much I owe and Meech not taking half. He want all of the money or me dead.

After Mercedes left the house I went and did some more hustling. I'm supposed to be able to chill and let other people handle this but for some reason, this shit was moving slower than the batch that came from Tez. His shit must be better than this batch I got from somebody else because the feins ain't biting fast enough. I guess that's why his shit was booming the way it did. I got the taste of what he was experiencing for about a week then it was back to square one. I'm mad as hell I got to give all this money to Meech. I don't know what I'm going to do now that I have another baby on the way, and Tori can't afford all of the bills and rent on her own so I still have to help her even if we're not going to be together.

I had so much shit on my mind right now that I can't focus. Usually I would talk to Rob about this kind of shit but he's gone. I can't even properly mourn him because don't nobody know he dead. His mother filed a missing person report a couple days after he died but the police don't have much to go on. I'm sure they're never going to find his body. His body is probably already at the bottom of somebody's ocean or worse.

After being at the trap for almost two hours, I only made two hundred dollars. That shit was depressing as hell. I was feeling like a pack worker all over again and I was selling my own shit. At this rate, I'm not going to be able to pay my workers the way that I'm supposed to. Once it gets to that point, I really don't know what to do.

I all but gave up and left the trap, driving to my mama's house. I needed to talk to her or my sister. Parking out front, I used my key and entered the house. Kelly and my mother were sitting on the couch watching TV.

"Hey y'all," I spoke.

"Hey baby," my mama replied.

"What are you doing here?" Kelly asked.

"I need to talk to y'all about something for a minute," I said, sitting on the love seat.

"You haven't been shot again, have you?" Kelly questioned, getting my mother's attention.

"Boy, when were you shot?" my mother countered.

"It was a couple weeks ago, but that's not what this is about. Well, it kind of is."

"Jermaine, what have you gotten yourself into?" my mother asked, worried.

I took a deep breath, trying to see where I wanted to start at. Everything I had to tell them was fucked up. I decided to tell them about my situation with Meech first and save Tori for last.

"Last month I ran into Kelvin. I was telling him about my money situation and he said he could set up a meeting with his boss. A couple weeks later he reached out and went to see his boss. I thought that he was going to put me on his team to sell drugs or something but instead, he wanted me to take care of a hit for him. The hit was for Tez's friend, Josh. He wanted to take Josh down so he could get to Tez. He was offering me, Rob, and Don thirty-five thousand dollars apiece, so I agreed. The plan was to do the hit then put our money together to start our own shit. Things didn't go quite as planned because Rob and Don both got killed. That's when I ran and ended up here with a bullet in my leg."

"Maine, tell me that you're not serious right now. Tell me that you did not try to kill your girlfriend's brother's people. Do you know what Tez will do to you if he finds out about this?" Kelly asked.

"Tez is the least of my worries right now. Meech found out that I stole a kilo of drugs and fifty thousand dollars from Tez's house. Now he's threatening to kill me if he don't get that money. I don't even have the money or drugs anymore. Then on top of that, Don and Rob both got killed at the house that day and there was nothing I could do about it. I could have called it in anonymously but I didn't have time because I had to run out the back door while Josh and his people were shooting at me."

"Ma, I told you that you missed out on some checks for this dumb nigga," Kelly said.

"So what are you going to do, Jermaine?" my mother inquired, ignoring my sister's comment.

"I've been working on trying to get the money back. I have half of the amount I stole but that doesn't make up for the other twenty-five thousand I took or the drugs. The dope I took was worth another thirty thousand dollars. I'm pretty much in a hole and I don't know how to get out of it."

"Did you try talking to Mercedes about this? Maybe she can talk to her brother," my mama suggested.

"Ma, I wish it was that easy. I can't tell Mercedes I stole from her brother. Plus, we're barely talking right now as it is. I didn't come home until morning two days in a row a couple days ago. One of the days I was with another woman and the next day was when I showed up here."

"Boy, I know you not cheating on that girl again after she's been taking care of your ass," my mama said.

"Yeah, but this time it's not all on me. Mercedes has changed since we first got together. She's talking back, drinking, smoking, and running the streets. She be having me feeling less of a man in the house with her. I'm always babysitting Makayla while she outside like I'm some kind of bitch."

"Good for Cedes. I wish her ass was here right now, I'd take her out for a drink to celebrate," Kelly stated.

"Who is this girl that you're dealing with? Do you love her?" my mama asked.

"No, I love Mercedes, it's just this weight loss has gone to her head. The girl I'm talking to name is Tori. I've been with her for almost seven months now. I kind of lied and told her I was only dealing with Mercedes because of our daughter. Now she's three months pregnant and she's keeping the baby. I put down a down payment for her a rental but with everything going on, I'm not going to be able to continue helping her."

"You're such a dumb ass nigga. After everything that Mercedes has done for you, your dumb ass go out and get another bitch pregnant. Let me get out of here before my fingers get the urge to call Mercedes' number," Kelly stated, getting up from the couch and walking to her room, leaving me and Mama alone.

"So what's your plan since you got a baby on the way with another woman? You're about to move in with the other woman now?"

"No, I'm still going to live with Mercedes. She doesn't

know about Tori or the baby. I'm just trying to find the right time to tell Tori that I lied about my relationship with Mercedes. I love her and I don't want to lose her."

"I'm sorry, but you should have thought about that when you was out sticking your dick in other women. Mercedes doesn't deserve the shit that you're doing behind her back. You need to leave that girl alone, because obviously she's not what you want and in the end, my grandbaby is going to end up being the one suffering."

"I would never do anything to hurt Makayla, and I love Mercedes. What happened with Tori was a mistake."

"That's bullshit and you know it, Jermaine. I raised your ass better than this. You're already hurting Makayla just by breaking up your family. As far as Tori goes, that's not a mistake. A mistake is doing it one time and regretting it so you stop. What you're doing is starting another relationship while you're already in one."

I ran my hands over my face because my mother was right. I needed another solution though that didn't involve me losing Makayla.

"Ma, I need you to tell me what to do."

"Well, first you need to figure out a way to get that money and quick, because Meech doesn't play. Next, you need to sit down with Mercedes and apologize for your fuck ups and then end the shit. Do you really think she about to play stepmama to a baby you had on her with another woman?"

"I don't know Ma, I need to go home and think about this. I'll see you later. Love you," I told her, standing up from my seat.

"I love you too," she said, hugging me tightly.

Leaving my mama's house, I had more questions than answers. The conversation with her was pointless because I'm not going to leave Mercedes. I really wish I could convince Tori to get rid of the baby. That would lessen my load because then Mercedes would never have to find out about my cheating because there would be no proof. I'm not even ready for another kid right now. I'm still getting used to being a father to Makayla and she's three. Maybe if the situation was different and I was financially stable, then I could entertain the idea.

When I pulled up to our apartment complex it was two in the morning and Mercedes' car wasn't outside. I parked my car then got out of the car and headed up the stairs. I went inside and grabbed a beer then sat down on the couch. I was tired but at the same time, I wanted to wait up for Mercedes. I wanted to talk to her and apologize for the bullshit I had been putting her through. I missed how our relationship used to be. We've argued more over these past few months than we have our entire relationship. Things were never supposed to be like this between us.

I waited up on the couch until almost three thirty and Mercedes still wasn't home yet. I tried calling her phone a couple times and didn't get an answer. Eventually I gave up and went to bed. I guess it was my turn to know how it feels when the person you love doesn't come home at night.

I woke up a few hours later around seven and the other side of the bed was empty. Climbing out of bed, I grabbed my keys and left the house. Getting in my car, I drove to Myra's house to see if Mercedes was there. Her car was parked out front but that didn't mean anything. She could be anywhere with anybody and just left her car there last night since she didn't drive it anyway. I debated on whether I was going to get out or just drive back home. Shit, I was here already so I might as well go knock on the door.

Parking my car behind Mercedes' car, I climbed out and walked up to the front door and rang the doorbell. It took a few minutes before someone finally came to the door.

"Jermaine, what the hell are you doing at my house at 7:30 in the morning?" Myra asked.

"Is Mercedes here? I got worried when she didn't come home last night."

"Well, now you know how she feels," Myra replied.

I hated that Mercedes had such a close relationship with her sister because she was always telling her our business.

"It's too early for this shit, Myra. Is she here or not?" I asked, getting irritated.

"Not, maybe she's out with her future husband right now," she said, closing the door in my face.

Hearing that made me angry as hell. I know there's no way that Mercedes been out fucking some other nigga all night. I know she's been upset with me but she wouldn't take it this far, would she? All kinds of crazy thoughts were going through my head right now.

I remained in the driveway for almost an hour to see if Mercedes was going to come out of the house or pull up with another nigga, but neither happened. Myra came and threatened to call the police for trespassing, so I cursed her out then pulled off and went back to the house to continue to wait on Mercedes. More and more she started making me feel like a bitch.

As I was walking in the house, my phone started to ring. I answered without looking at the screen, hoping that it was Mercedes, but it was Tori's voice on the other end of the phone.

"Good morning baby, are you coming over today?" Tori asked.

"I'm not sure, my baby mama went out last night and she ain't brought her ass home. Now I'm stuck here with the baby."

"Ugh, I hate the way your baby mama be doing you. You need to just come on and move with me now and you can go to court for rights for your daughter. She can't continue to hold your daughter over your head. You have every right to her as she does."

"I know, this is all just an adjustment that we're working on. Once school starts in a couple I can move out of here and in with you. She won't need me to watch our daughter as much because she's going to work around her schedule.

"Ugh, a couple months seem so long."

"It'll be here before you know it."

"Okay, hopefully she gets there soon so you can come over. I miss you."

"I miss you too," I replied.

We stayed on the phone for a few more minutes before hanging up. I was starting to feel restless so I went back to bed. I woke up to the sound of some bumping. Looking up, I saw Mercedes standing at her drawer looking for clothes. Her hair was wet so that meant she had just taken a shower. Now why would she need to take a shower as soon as she got in the house? Was she just washing that nigga's nut from between her legs? Rage instantly set in as my thoughts played tricks with me.

"Where the hell you been all night, Mercedes? It's almost noon," I said, looking at the clock.

"Do I question you when you're out doing your dirt?" she asked.

Her question threw me off for a minute because now I was wondering was she admitting to doing dirt or if all of these scenarios just have to do with my own guilt.

"I'm not about to play with your ass. Where you been?"

Mercedes rolled her eyes at me before finally answering.

"I was at Myra's house."

"Don't fucking lie to me. I went to her house and she said you wasn't there."

"She was just bullshitting with you. I was in the guest room sleep."

"Why didn't you come home last night?"

Mercedes had a look of irritation on her face, but I didn't give a fuck. I had questions and only she had the answers. Asking her had to be a lot safer than my assumptions.

"We didn't leave the club until almost four. After that we went to Waffle House for breakfast. By then it was almost six and I was too tired to drive so I went to sleep at her house," Mercedes explained.

I looked at her for a minute and it didn't look like she was lying.

"Had you let me drop you off and pick you up, you wouldn't have had that problem."

"I didn't have a problem with anything. I enjoyed my night to the fullest," she stated, climbing in bed next to me.

"If you went to sleep at your sister's house, why are you getting in bed right now? Don't you have to go get our daughter?"

"Look, chill out with all the questions. You really starting to blow my high right now. You got me feeling like I'm being interrogated or some shit. Just ask the question that you really want the answer to so that we can get this shit over with," she said.

"Did you fuck somebody else last night?" I asked, hoping I didn't end up regretting asking the question.

"No I didn't, but I could have," she replied.

"What is that supposed to mean?" I asked, sitting up in the bed at that point.

"It means I met somebody that wanted to get to know me better. Somebody that's willing to show me attention, but I turned him down because I'm with you. Although I've been questioning that decision damn near every day for the past two weeks now. I need you to give me a reason as to why I should remain in this relationship with you."

I knew that she was really tired of my shit if she admitted to meeting somebody else. If he was at the party for Bryce he was most likely a nigga with money too.

"I'm sorry for everything I've been putting you through lately. I've just been stressing about money and our living situation. This isn't the type of place I wanted our daughter to grow up in. Everything seemed like it was going easy and then suddenly I took a hit. By then I had already bought the car."

"Why won't you just get a job then, Maine? If I have to do this on my own, what do I need you for? I can get dick from anybody if sex is the only thing being offered to me."

"Okay, I'll go out tomorrow and look for one. I'm going to do better, I promise. Please don't leave me," I pleaded.

When she didn't say anything, I climbed on top of her. I know she said that she wasn't out fucking, but I wanted to see for myself. I know how her pussy feels so I'll be able to tell if another dick been where it didn't belong last night.

"Jermaine, move please, I'm trying to take a nap before Myra brings Kayla home," she whined.

I ignored her request and started placing kisses on her neck. My fingers slipped into her underwear, playing on her clit. The feeling soon took over her body and she couldn't get her words out. Mercedes turned her head to face me, allowing me to kiss her. The kiss started off slow then it intensified, and I started sucking on her tongue. She wrapped her legs around me as my fingers moved faster. She used her feet to push my boxers down and soon my hard member was poking her entrance. I looked down at her, smirking as I rubbed the tip around her entrance.

I knew this was going to drive her crazy. If she turned me down after this, that meant she was a bold face lie and she's been giving my pussy away. The crazy thing about it is that I would still forgive her if that was the case because I drove her to do it.

Maine, come on," she moaned.

"What, babe? You want this dick?"

She nodded her head, wiggling up under me.

"Nah, I need you to use your words."

"I want you to fuck me, babe," she purred, biting on her bottom lip.

I slowly slid inside of her wetness and we both moaned in pleasure. I didn't have a big ass dick but I was a good seven inches with a curve and I knew how to handle it. My pace was slow and Mercedes ran her hands all over my back, digging her nails into it. It was her way of marking her territory. If I took my shirt off in front of another bitch, they would see the scratches on my back.

"Ahhhh Maine, that shit feel so good, baby," she moaned.

I loved hearing her call out my name. I sped up the pace, going deeper. Mercedes' moans got louder and both of us were close to climaxing. Her legs shook and my body jerked as we came together.

We stayed in bed for almost two hours pleasing each other. This wasn't something new to us but it was something that we hadn't done in a while. As of lately, whenever we had sex it was a quick wham bam thank you ma'am. We no longer took out the time to make sure we were pleasing each other properly.

The way Mercedes was fucking me today had me scared. I couldn't tell if it was her way of forgiving me or if she was getting it all out of her system and I was never going to slide between her thighs again. Either way, I was going to enjoy every moment of it and not ruin it with words.

CHAPTER EIGHT
MARTEZ

A month has passed since Meech robbed my trap, and the time for me to strike back was finally here. I've done surveillance of the warehouse for the past month and like clockwork, everything was the same. There were ten men rotating in and out of the building. That meant no matter what time of day it was, there was going to be ten men inside the building. That was something I could handle.

From what I can tell, the only time Meech goes to the warehouse is when they have a shipment come in, which was this morning. For that reason alone, tonight is the perfect time to knock them across their heads. If I steal the shipment that just came in today, that's going to hurt his pockets and it's going to look bad for business. I wouldn't even be doing this if he'd just leave me alone. I don't fuck with nobody at all.

The only thing I do is get my money and stay in the cut. I'm a self-made millionaire and I can't even enjoy the fruits of my labor. My mother benefits off of it but that's about it. I do shit for Myra here and there, but she don't need it because I pay Bryce well just because he's in a relationship with my sister. I would love to at least let Mercedes enjoy the shit, but she won't do right. If she leave that nigga Jermaine alone she wouldn't have to lift a finger unless she wanted to. I'd go out tomorrow and buy her whatever house she wanted and furnish it completely.

My sister is beautiful as hell and can do better than Jermaine. I don't give a fuck that she had a baby with him. It's plenty of niggas out here ready to play stepdaddy to Makayla. I know this for a fact because some of them done hit me up out of respect, asking if it was alright to talk to her. I have to tell them all that she's in love with a lame right now so she ain't going. Hopefully she come to her senses soon and leaves his ass.

Jermaine has never done anything to me, but his vibe has been off to me since day one. A lot of it has to do with the fact that he was twenty-one years old and got my seventeen-year-old sister pregnant. When I found that shit out, I was hot as fuck. It took my mama to talk me down from killing that nigga. He knew he was foul as hell for even fucking with her let alone getting her pregnant. That was the first time that me and Mercedes ever had a fall out.

I tried convincing Mercedes to move in with me when I found out she was pregnant, but she told me she was moving in with Jermaine and his family. That was one of the dumbest decisions she could have made. I didn't understand why she would choose his family over hers. I was ready to question my sister's loyalty until my mother explained to me that it wasn't about loyalty.

Mercedes was a young woman trying to figure life out. She needed to be able to make her own mistakes and I had to allow it. That was the only way that she would learn to grow and be independent. I listened to my mother and took a step back. That was one of the hardest things I've ever done because I never wanted my sister to struggle. I waited for her to give me the word or ask for help, but she never did it.

I damn near caved and bought her a house when she moved in that damn apartment she lives in, in College Park. She ain't know shit about living in the hood. My daddy made sure that none of us grew up in the hood. He bought a house for all of our mothers far away from the hood. He always said you don't shit where you eat. That's why my house is in a lowkey area. I learned my lesson three years ago when I used to have parties and bitches at my crib.

One day a bitch set me up and I almost lost my life. Three niggas ran up in my shit and tried to rob me. Luckily I had an expensive ass security system and was quick on my feet. None of them lived to tell the day about running up in my shit. After that I went and bought the house I live in now. I made a vow that only the people I trust with my life would know where I live. That's why the only people that's been in my house is Myra, Mercedes, my mama, Josh, and my nieces. I know that none of them would ever crack under pressure and tell where I live. Hell, they never even told the niggas that they live with where I live.

At first Kaye had a problem with not knowing where I live. I told her out the gate that wasn't changing until I put a ring on her finger, and I meant that shit. I got her an apartment in Buckhead so I could meet up with her there. As long as she had a roof over her head and I was coming to visit her, she didn't need to know where I live. I feel like once she knows where I live her ass will randomly start popping up at my house to see if I'm where I say I am. I've been through crazy already and I'm not going through that shit again. That was another reason why I stopped telling females where I live.

I used to catch one of my exes driving up and down my street trying to see if I was home or if someone was there with me. I had a garage so she was never going to see someone's car outside my house. She used to sit out front and then call my phone to see if I answer or time how long it took. The bitch was acting like a psycho and I had to threaten her family for her to leave me alone.

When I pulled up to the warehouse there were cars parked outside. My niggas was on time just like I expected. I had some of the realest goons on my team and they all respected me. I didn't have to put fear in their hearts to make them loyal to me. I don't have to yell or do dumb shit to put them in their place. I make sure they want to work for me. I look out for them and their families on a regular. If I'm eating, my workers eating too. I don't make them work for pennies and have to struggle to feed their families.

When a man doesn't have a way to feed their family it causes them to do desperate shit. That's when you have to worry about them robbing you or setting you up. The people that work for me at this level are the same men that were there when I first got in the game. They all grew and built with me so it was only right that I looked out for them. They proved their loyalty just by following me when I didn't know what the fuck I was doing. They could have left when Stephen got locked up but they chose to stay and work up under me. It's been a journey for all of us but we made it through it.

Putting the code in, I entered the warehouse and spoke to my security as I walked down the hall to my office. I went inside and went into my closet, grabbing my black duffle bag. I pulled out my all-black hit clothes. I always wore a pair of cargo pants, t-shirt, hoodie, mask, and gloves. I got dressed and put on everything right now except for the mask and gloves. I don't put those on until I make it to my location.

I locked my office back up and walked to the meeting room. All of the men were sitting around the long table talking, but once they saw me they immediately stopped what they were doing and stood to their feet. Giving them a head nod of acknowledgment, they sat back down. They were all suited and booted, ready to get this shit done. This was pretty much how our routine went when we had hits or business to take care of. They would be in the conference room thirty minutes before the meeting, waiting until I showed up.

"What's up y'all, we don't have a long time. I just want to run through this one more time then we can go," I said, nodding toward Josh so he could do the run down.

"Okay, so as we know, there will be ten guys inside of the building. It's going to be sixteen of us all together. We're taking two vans and there will be eight of us in each one. When we get to the warehouse the drivers will stay in the van. The four snipers will be on the roof watching all the angles for covers. Then the other ten of us will be going in. There's three entrances and we'll be splitting into three groups. Once inside you all know your position and what you're supposed to do," Josh explained.

"Do you all have any questions?" I asked.

Everybody shook their head, so there was nothing else to discuss. There was no need for me to point out how important this was because they already knew. I also didn't need to tell them not to fuck up because they're always on their shit and down for whatever. I dismissed the guys and they had ten minutes to call whoever they needed to before we leave.

One of the things we always did was reach out to our loved ones when we did shit like this because there was no guarantee that we were going to make it out of this alive. We also leave our cell phones behind. I trust my people but at the same time, I can't be stupid or get caught slipping. I'd like to think my people would always remain loyal to me but at the same time, I'm at war with my uncle, so that says a lot.

Ten minutes later we all exited the warehouse and got in our assigned vehicles. Me and Josh never ride in the same vehicle when we hit the streets because if some shit goes down, at least one of has to be around to handle the business. Say for instance if police pull us over. We can't both be going to jail together. Who gone take over for me then? These are the kind of things I have to look at on a daily basis. I am working on training someone up under Josh right now because once I retire, he will need a right hand.

We piled up in the van and Ant pulled off. It took almost an hour to get to Meech's warehouse. The entire ride was silent because I needed my people focused with no distractions. Ant parked out of the camera's view and killed the engine. I put on my ski mask, night vision glasses, and gloves then grabbed the guns from the duffle bag. I double checked the clips before we all climbed out.

I waited for the signal that the electricity was cut. Once that was confirmed I led the way to the warehouse. Everyone went to their assigned spot, then we breeched the building. We went inside guns blazing and the niggas didn't know what hit them.

My men started putting the money and dope in bags while the rest of us took the men out one by one. Turning the lights off caught them off guard, so they didn't even get a chance to shoot back, which was a plus for us. I'm assuming since they're in the warehouse they don't keep their guns by them. That right there is a rookie move because I'm always strapped. Even when I'm fucking my bitch the gun is on the nightstand in arm's reach. My biggest fear has always been to get taken out while I'm knee deep in some pussy. I heard stories about that all the time and said that could never be me.

I smiled as I shot three of the niggas in less than two minutes. This killing shit was easy and came naturally to me. If

I was to ever have a drought in this dope shit, I could be a professional hit man. I'd charge half a milli a body and it would be worth every penny. All they needed to do was tell me how they wanted it done and I'd make it happen.

Now that I think about it, I should start a business for contract killers. I would put a group of gunmen on my payroll, then I'd set up contracts and each bounty would be a different amount. I would send it to them and they have the option of doing the job or not. Everything would be done through an app with the click of a button. I loved the idea so I pushed it to the back of my mind and finished what I came here for.

We were in and out in fifteen minutes with no issues. Hurriedly, we ran back to the vans and took off heading back to the warehouse. Once we were there we went inside and got changed then I did a quick debrief. Since everything went accordingly, there wasn't much for me to say. I wasn't going to make them stay behind and count. We'd do all of that shit tomorrow.

I left the warehouse and headed to Kaye's crib, even though I didn't feel like it. I was tired as fuck and ready to climb in my bed. I needed at least four hours of sleep to rejuvenate but I haven't seen her in a couple of weeks and I told her I would stop by tonight.

I pulled up to her apartment building and parked in the garage then headed upstairs. Using my key, I entered and found her lying on the couch sleeping peacefully. My baby was beautiful as hell. She could have been a model if she wanted to. She was tall with legs for days with smooth almond skin, dark brown eyes, and pearly white teeth. She had just enough ass for me to grip a hand full and D-cup breasts. Even though she was no longer stripping she prided herself in taking care of her body. She worked out and ate right on a regular.

I bent down and kissed her on the cheek, causing her to

wake up. She looked up at me with a broad smile like I was her favorite person in the world. Jumping up from the couch, she wrapped her arms around me and hugged me tight. My baby really did miss me. I was going to have to find time to be able to take her out on a date soon.

"Hey baby," I spoke.

"Heyyyy, you came," she replied.

"I told you that I would," I said, grabbing her hand leading her to the bedroom.

With no words being said, I stripped out of my clothes and she wasted no time dropping to her knees. She wrapped her lips around my dick and my right hand instantly went to the back of her head. I held onto the back of it as she did her thing. The shit was feeling good as hell and I was getting weak in the knees.

On the verge of cumming, I pulled out of her mouth and threw her on the bed. I would have loved to cum in her mouth but the truth was, as tired as I was, I wasn't sure if my shit would get back hard to fuck.

Since she was already wet from sucking me off, I inserted myself into her slowly, causing a moan to escape both of our lips. I kissed her deep as our fingers intertwined. I started to push in more and my heartrate picked up as I felt how wet her pussy was. It had been a couple weeks since we fucked and it was taking everything in me not to bust early. I didn't want to disappoint her after making her wait all of this time.

I continued making love to her nice and slow until she came on my dick, causing my shit to jerk. It was enough of the slow shit now. Flipping her over, I plunged my dick in her, causing her to scream out as I gave her long and deep strokes. She was screaming and trying to run.

"Take this dick and stop playing with me. This is what you

wanted, right?" I asked, grabbing a hand full of her hair as her ass bounced against me.

"Yesss, Tez, wait baby. Please, you're sooo deep," she screamed.

"Fuck, you should see the way my dick look going in and out of you."

My shit was glistening from her cum, causing me to want to stay in the pussy even longer. I could feel my nut ready to come but I held that shit back. She tried moving again so I trapped her legs in between mine.

"Tez, I'm about to cum again," she moaned.

"Well come on this shit then," I demanded, slapping her on the ass.

She started gushing everywhere, pushing my dick out. I waited for her to finish then slid right back in. All you heard was her screams and moans throughout the room. It was good that we had thick walls or the neighbors would definitely hear what we had going on.

After another ten minutes of straight fucking, I pulled out and nutted in my hand. She was on birth control but we could never be too safe. Climbing out of bed, I grabbed her hand and led her to the bathroom. We took a shower and then got in bed together.

Laying down naked, I pulled her close to me.

"I love you," Kaye said.

"I love you, babe. I'm going to need you to chill with that jealous shit. Your pussy is the only one that I want. This dick belongs to you. I promise it's not going to be like this forever. I just need you to continue to be patient with me."

"I will, I'm sorry for how I reacted earlier. I was just frustrated."

"It's cool, your man is tired so let's get some sleep."

I closed my eyes and instantly fell asleep. The sound of my

phone woke me up about three hours later and it felt like I hadn't closed my eyes. Looking down at the phone, I saw Meech's name come across my screen. This motherfucker was so predictable that it made no sense. I was starting to wonder how he survived this long in the game.

"What's up Unc," I answered.

"Nigga, don't play with me. Where the fuck is my product and money?"

"I don't know what you talking about," I replied. There was no way in hell I was going to talk about this shit over the phone. He could be working for the feds for all I know and I'm not about to incriminate me or my team.

"Look, you wanted to talk and you made your point. Where do you want to meet up at?" he asked, trying to reason with me.

"Shit, it's too late to talk now," I told him, hanging up the phone.

He instantly called right back and I picked up on the first ring.

"Yo," I answered.

"Nigga, if I don't get my shit back within the next twenty-four hours, my sister is going to be burying your bitch ass next to your daddy," he threatened me.

"Motherfucker, you know where to find me," I said, hanging up again.

After that conversation, I wasn't going to be able to get back to sleep so I got up and got dressed. I told Kaye I had to go. Of course, she had a slight attitude but I didn't have time to deal with it right now. I didn't have the luxury to be able to lay up during war. I needed to get back to the warehouse and sort everything out. I also needed to sit down with my sisters because they were going to have to lay low temporarily until all of this is taken care of.

CHAPTER NINE

JERMAINE

It's been a couple weeks since I've seen Makayla and Mercedes. Montez and Meech is in a full-out war right now so he has them tucked away at a safe house with Myra and the kids. I talk to Mercedes every day but I don't know her location. Tez and Josh are the only two people that know where they're staying at. The bright side of all of that is since Meech is paying so much attention to Tez, he's not threatening me anymore.

I'm not crazy enough to think he's going to drop the situation. It does give me more time to come up with the money though. Instead of me just trying to sell all of my product on my own, I started working with this nigga Rome. I've been making moves for him and my money has been consistent.

I checked the address that I wrote down, making sure that I was at the correct house before grabbing the duffle bag and getting out of the car. I walked up the walkway then rang the doorbell. I waited for about a minute and when no one answered, I rang the doorbell again. I was standing out here with all this dope and they wanted to take their slow ass time coming to the door.

A couple minutes later, the front door opened and some woman appeared.

"Who are you? Where's Ralph?" I asked, annoyed.

"He had to make a run but he asked me to get the delivery from you."

"I don't know about that. I was only supposed to leave it with him," I replied skeptically.

"Do you want this thirty thousand or not?" she asked, pulling out three stacks of cash.

Shit, she got the right amount of money so Ralph must've left it for her to give to me. If not, that was between them. As long as I got my money, that's all that counts.

"Here," I said, handing her the drugs and taking the money.

I left the house as quick as I came and headed to Rome's spot. I parked out front and got out of the car, entering his main spot. This was where the money was counted and crack was cooked. He had six bitches that worked out of here. He was on some *New Jack City* type of shit. Bitches was walking around butt ass naked with masks on their face. Some of them were in the living room counting money. You went to another room and they were cutting crack, and you went to the kitchen they were cooking it.

The only thing Rome did was sit back in a chair supervising everything. Oh, and get his dick sucked by different women. He literally sits there in front of everybody while he gets head. The other females just continue working until it's their turn.

"What's up, man? You took care of that?"

"Yeah, but it was some bitch at the house. She said Ralph was away but she gave me the thirty thousand," I said, handing it to him.

"Cool, here's your cut," he said, handing me five thousand dollars.

"Thanks, same time tomorrow?" I asked.

"You can come back tomorrow, but let me ask you a question. Why you only want to do runs at seven? You know if you did more during the day you could be making triple that amount."

"I know, I'll probably change it soon. Right now I got hella shit going on in my life and I'm just trying to keep my head above water," I replied.

"Okay, well I'll get at you tomorrow."

I dapped Rome up then left the house. Sticking the five thousand in my trunk, I got in the car and pulled off. I needed a haircut bad as hell so I headed to the barber shop. It was a Wednesday evening so it wasn't as crowded. I sat in my regular barber Kyle's chair and he immediately started talking shit about my head.

"Nigga, why you ain't been come in here to get this shit cut? You out here walking around looking like wolf man."

"Man, shit has been crazy. I've been trying to work on my relationship and then ole girl I was creeping with is pregnant and she not getting rid of it. I'm basically trying to take care of two households at the same time. I already got one kid that I was barely able to take care of, now I'm about to have another one."

"Damn man, that's fucked up. Your pull-out game that weak," Kyle laughed.

"Nigga, that shit not funny at all. I thought I was going to fall the fuck out when I found out about ole girl having a baby."

"Your girl must don't know yet."

"Hell nah, I'm scared to find out what she would do if she does find out because she's been real quiet lately. It's like the calm before the storm at my crib."

Me and Kyle chopped it up until he finished cutting my hair. I gave him two twenty-dollar bills then left out. As I was walking to my car, I spotted a black car with dark tints driving slowly in my direction. Screams erupted as gunfire came out of nowhere. My brain automatically went to fight or flight mode. I didn't have anywhere to hide at because I was in the middle of the road, so I started shooting back until their truck ran into a parked car. The shooting I've been doing at the range paid off.

Hurriedly, I jumped in my car and sped away until I was out of the area, then I drove the normal speed. I was going straight in the house and staying in all night. I was kind of wishing I could go into hiding with Mercedes. I guess Meech was capable of going to war with Montez and me at the same time. I parked my car and went inside of the building. When I made it to the second floor landing, I had to pause for a minute to make sure I was seeing right.

"Tori, what the hell are you doing here?" I asked, looking around.

"Well, you haven't came to see me in a week and you're not answering your phone, so I wanted to make sure you were good."

"I'm good, now you can go," I told her as I opened the front door. The last thing I needed was for one of the neighbors to see her at my house and it gets back to Mercedes.

"Don't be rude, it took me almost forty minutes to get here. The least you can do is invite me in so I can meet your baby mama. This conversation is well overdue."

"My baby mama not here. She's out of town right now."

"Good, that's even better," she stated, pushing past me.

I've been missing Mercedes like crazy, but this is the one time I'm so damn grateful that she's away. Reluctantly, I closed the door behind me and entered the house.

"How do you know where I live?" I asked.

"I took a peek at your registration and saw the address," she confessed.

"Okay, now that you saw I was good, you need to go," I told her.

"I thought you said your baby mama was gone out of town," she said, pulling her sundress over her head, revealing her naked body. She didn't have on any underwear up under it. I guess since it was hot she was giving her cat some air.

"We can't do this here," I told her.

"Why not? You said you're not with your baby mama anymore and I'm your woman. I want some dick and I know you not about to turn me down," she stated, walking away.

I locked the front door and grabbed a bottle of water. By the time I made it to the room, she was lying in bed with her legs wide open, playing in her pussy. I wanted to yell at her to get the fuck out, but my dick was already standing at attention.

I took off my clothes and climbed in bed next to her. Without hesitating, she climbed on top of my dick and started moving her hips in a circular motion. Her titties was bouncing up and down as she was putting in work. I held onto her waist and started fucking her from the bottom. She was making all kind of sex faces and biting on her bottom lip. No lie, that shit was turning me on.

I flipped her over and started hitting it from the back, watching her ass jiggle and clap. Grabbing onto a handful of her hair, I went deeper, hitting her spot until she was cumming again.

"Oh my god, baby, that shit feels so good," she cried out as she gushed all over me again.

I slapped her on the ass one more time before laying down on my back.

"Ride this dick until I nut up in that pussy," I demanded.

"Your wish is my command, daddy." She smiled before climbing back on top of me. She rode my dick nice and slow this time. All you could hear was our moans through the room. I was on the verge of cumming until I heard Tori cry out and she was no longer on my dick. I was about to ask what happened until I saw Mercedes dragging her by the hair. When Tori hit the floor, Cedes started punching her in the face.

"Babe, wait!" I yelled, pulling her up off of Tori. Even though I didn't want the baby, I didn't want it to die like this and I didn't need Cedes going to jail.

"Get the fuck off of me, Maine. How the fuck could you bring another bitch to my house and fuck her in the bed that we share? That our daughter lays in with us? I give you chance after chance and each time all you do is fuck me over. I'm so over you and this relationship. I literally have been giving you the benefit of the doubt. Everybody has been telling me how stupid I am to still be with you and I just don't listen. They were right all along. Get your bitch and get the fuck out of my house," she yelled.

I was about to respond when there was a loud bang at the front door, getting all of our attention. My first thought was that it was Meech's people, so I grabbed my gun.

"Y'all wait here," I told them, walking out of the room naked. I didn't have time to put on clothes. Of course, Mercedes' hard headed ass didn't pay me any attention.

When we made it to the living room, the door was busted down and there were police with guns out.

"POLICE, PUT THE GUN DOWN NOW. GET ON THE FLOOR!" one of the officers screamed, pointing his gun at us.

Mercedes' lips quivered as she got on the floor, and I followed behind her. Tori came running from the back and immediately dropped to the floor as well. The police started searching the place without saying anything.

"Can you tell us what you're doing here? I asked.

"Yes, Jermaine Mann, you're under arrest for drug trafficking, distribution, and a person of interest in a shooting that took place today at a barber shop on Peachtree," the officer stated.

All I could do was hold my head low because I was caught. Even if they didn't have proof of the drugs, I was just caught red handed with a gun.

"Can I at least put on clothes?" I asked.

"Yeah, one of the young ladies can get clothes for you," he replied.

I looked over at Mercedes, causing her to roll her eyes at me before getting up from the floor. She came back about a couple minutes later with a pair of boxers, a t-shirt, and a pair of joggers.

I stood from the floor and got dressed before one of the officers cuffed me. This shit was awkward as hell, but I guess it was my Karma for all the shit I had done catching up with me. Not only did Mercedes catching me cheating, but the police show up right after? Then to top it off, I didn't even get my nut off.

When I made it to the police station I was taken into booking. They fingerprinted me then I was taken into the interrogation room where I was questioned for almost two more hours. The shit I was caught up in didn't have to do with Meech or my own shit. It had to do with Rome's organization. The feds had been watching his ass for years and my dumb ass got caught right in the middle of the shit. The icing on the cake was when I served that woman today. She was an undercover agent, so I couldn't even lie about not knowing what was going on. I knew I should have walked away when it took all that time for somebody to come to the door.

The officers also told me that two people died and there

were five injuries at the barbershop shooting. If my slugs matched any of the ones they pulled from the bodies, I was fucked. I knew I was going to have to do time regardless, but I need a good ass lawyer to try and help decrease it. If I ended up with a public defender, I was good as gone. They asses are overbooked and underpaid. Not to mention they work for the state, so all of that is bullshit to me.

After about another hour of interrogation, the officer allowed me to make my phone call. I dialed Mercedes' number because I was going to need her to call my lawyer and get the money to pay the fees. I had about fifty thousand dollars saved up. I was going to use it to pay Meech, but now that I'm going to end up in jail, none of that shit matters now.

"Hello," she answered on the third ring.

"Hey, it's me. I don't have long to talk. I need you to do me a favor. I have a bail hearing in the morning at nine and it's not looking good. I know I'll have to use a public defender for that because I know it's going to be hard to find a lawyer now since it's late. So tomorrow I need you to find a good defense attorney and hire him for me. There's a safe under the bed and the code is 1008. It should be enough in there to get him started on my case."

"Okay," she said and then hung up the phone on me.

I guess I shouldn't have expected her to talk to me after what just happened. There was no need to talk about it right now anyway, and it wasn't like I could talk my way out of it. She literally caught me right in the middle of the act. If I could do things differently with my life, I would. My greatest mistake was fucking over the woman that showed me unconditional love.

CHAPTER TEN

MERCEDES

Today I woke up with a feeling in the pit of my stomach that something was wrong. I tried to brush the feeling off but it just wouldn't leave. My first mind went to Montez since he was beefing with his damn uncle. That got to be the dumbest shit ever, but I'm not involved in street shit so I don't know what that's all about. It's not my business so I don't ask any questions. Montez always says the less we know the better.

We've been hiding out at his house for the past two weeks. At first he was going to send us out of town, but he wanted us somewhere that he could get to us if he needed to. It's not like anybody knew where he lived, and he hired around-the-clock security. He got the outside of his house looking like Fort Wayne. I've been enjoying spending time with Myra and the kids.

Montez has a big ass game room and movie theater in his house with a swimming pool out back, so we have more than enough to entertain us. Me and Myra both needed more clothes and stuff for the kids, so we convinced Montez to let us go to the house. He only agreed if we rode together and with security.

The driver dropped me off and then went to drop Myra off. Once she was done they were going to come back and get me, which was fine because I needed to have a conversation with Jermaine. I was about to end things with him because I felt like we were just going with the motion at this point.

I had one foot in and one foot out of my relationship and I was ready to step all the way out. I also had been talking to Rio and I didn't feel comfortable going past the talking stage while I was still with Maine. No matter how much dirt he did, I couldn't allow myself to stoop to his level. I wouldn't feel right doing that and Rio has been patient with me.

That night when we all left the club, Myra gave him my number just like she said she would. He went out to breakfast with us and then back to Bryce's house. We went to the guest room and just chilled. We talked for hours and then afterward, he took me out to eat again. Once I got back, I got in my car and drove back home. Thoughts of Rio were on my mind the entire time, even when I got in the shower. I pleasured myself thinking about him and was ready to pass out. That's when Jermaine decided he wanted to fuck. I was hot and bothered so I slept with him, but it felt so wrong afterward because I was wishing that it was Rio fucking me.

That was the last time that we had sex because that same evening is when Montez told me I had twenty minutes to pack a bag for me and Makayla. He told me not to ask any questions so I didn't. I just did what my brother asked and left. Later on that night, Jermaine came home to an empty house, calling to see where I was. I told him I was away with Myra and the kids but those were the only details I could give.

The plan was when I came to see Jermaine today, after we talked, I was going to find a middle point for him to meet me so that he could spend some time with Makayla. Even though I no longer wanted to be with him, that didn't mean he couldn't spend time with his daughter. I wanted to end things on good terms and coparent since I loved him. That shit was too much like right though.

When I walked in the house, I saw a dress on the floor that didn't belong to me, so that was strike number one. As I walked toward the bedroom, I heard moaning, which was strike two. I was hoping that Jermaine was watching a porn and not dumb enough to have a bitch in my house. Strike three was when I stepped foot in my bedroom and a bitch was riding his dick. I instantly blacked out and pulled her up off of him.

I always said that I would confront my nigga and not the other female because she owed me no loyalty. This situation was different though, because I caught them fucking in my bed. There's no way she didn't know a woman lived here with the way my house was decorated. There was fucking picture of me, Maine, and Makayla on the fucking bedroom wall.

Once Jermaine pulled me off of that ho, I was about to tear in his ass. He's so lucky the police showed up or his ass would have been on his way to the hospital instead. I was going to get my gun from my safe and shoot his ass right in his dick since he couldn't keep it in his pants.

Jermaine's bitch was scared as hell when the police took him away. She standing here crying and looking like a fool, talking about what do we do now. I told her ass I don't give a fuck what she do but it better be outside my house. She ran out so damn fast after that you would have thought she was the road runner.

I called Myra and told her what happened. She dropped everything she was doing and had the driver bring her back to my house. I had to call the building management so that someone could come out and fix the door. I already knew someone was going to be calling me tomorrow and ready to kick me out. I'm cool with that because now that Jermaine's out of the picture, I'm going to let Tez get me my own place. I know he's going to want me to wait until everything dies down, which is fine by me. I don't have a problem staying at his house. He's barely there anyway to begin with.

It took maintenance a couple of hours to come and fix my door. By that time, me and Myra had packed me and Kayla's stuff in some suitcases. I'd just get Montez to get some of his people to pack up the rest of the house and put my stuff in storage until I move into another place. We were just about to leave the house when an unknown number showed up on my phone. Usually I don't answer them but I thought, what the hell.

When I heard Jermaine's voice on the other end, I was about to hang up on his ass but I decided to listen. When he mentioned a safe my ears perked up. I made sure to make a mental note of the code since it was our daughter's birthday. I told him okay and hung up the phone. He had me fucked up if he thought I was about to search for him a lawyer. Had I not just caught him fucking another bitch, I would've done it for him. Now that's his new bitch's job.

I slid the safe from up under the bed and put in the code. Opening it up, I saw racks of money. Grabbing it all, I stuck it inside of an empty duffle bag. I'd count it when I got to Tez's house since Myra is outside waiting on me. I grabbed my purse and locked the door before walking out of my apartment for the last time. I was about to close one chapter of my life and start a new one.

I got in the back seat with Myra and we rode in silence to the house. I wanted to cry so bad but my tears wouldn't escape my eyes. It was like they knew Jermaine wasn't worth my tears. I was going to end things with him because I was catching feelings for another man, but it's not the same thing. Rio is somebody that I'm just getting to know. That bitch that Maine was with is something that's been ongoing. I could tell from the way she was crying. Her ass is in love with that nigga so she can have his jailbird ass. Me and mine gone be alright, and I hope he don't think I'm going to bring Kayla to visit him, because that's not happening.

When we pulled up to the house, Pete told us to go inside and he'd get some of the guys to help bring my stuff in. I thanked him then entered the house. I went upstairs to the girls' room to check on them. They both were knocked out sleep and I was grateful for that. I wasn't in the mood to parent right now. Right now I needed to get drunk and cry on my sister's shoulder.

Walking out of the room, I closed the door and headed downstairs. Myra already had sad hoe music playing and a bottle of Patrón in her hand. I grabbed some lime and salt then we sat down and starting taking shots. Neither of us said a word and I was fine with that. When Vivian Green's "Gotta Go Gotta Leave" came on, I started singing along with it. By the time it was at the end of the song, I was singing at the top of my lungs.

Now I take the blame
For trying to stay and work it out
Shoulda left before it got complicated
Shoulda left when there was still some happiness

Yes I take the blame
For having faith in the relationship
I thought it made me complete

But the truth is
I'm complete without it
Yeah-eah
(Gotta Let Go-ooo-ooo-oo)

[Chorus]
I gotta go. I gotta leave
So please don't make it hard for me
I've gave enough, I'm tired of love
I gotta let it go...

I swear Vivian was talking her shit in that song. That's exactly how I was feeling right now. Had I broke things off with Jermaine six months ago when I started to, things could be so different right now. We would probably have had a shot at being friends. Now it was going to take a while for me to forgive him and even then, his ass is in jail and there's no telling how long he's going to be in there. Things could have been so different and he just had to fuck it up, then got the nerve to ask me to go find him a lawyer. That nigga was sitting on all that money and didn't give a dime for me or my baby. Everything was starting to make sense now. The car, clothes, coming and going all kinds of night. He got me fucked up if he thinks I'm going to use that money for a lawyer. That money is my retribution for putting up with his shit for all of these years.

Halfway through the bottle of Patrón, me and Myra were both singing and crying. I didn't know what the hell her ass was crying for. I'm guessing it was just her feeding off of my emotions, because there wasn't a damn thing wrong with her.

"What's wrong with y'all?" Montez asked, walking into the living room sitting next to us.

I laid my head on my brother's shoulder and broke down crying. This was the only time I've allowed him to see me cry besides when my father died, because he be ready to kill shit. I guess this time I let it show since Jermaine is locked up and he can't get to him. He may be a piece of shit but he's still Makayla's dad, and cheating is equivalent to death.

"Calm down, baby girl, and tell me what's wrong. I can't help you if you don't tell me," Montez told me, kissing me on my forehead.

"I walked in on Jermaine fucking another girl in our bed. After that, the police kicked in my door and took him to jail. Something about drug trafficking and a shootout by a barbershop."

"I'm sorry, what can I do? You want me to go bail him out so you can go shoot him?" he asked seriously.

"No, it's all good. I just need to drink and take a long, hot bath before getting a good night's sleep."

"Okay, well first, y'all going to have to eat something. I'm going to order some food and go change then I'll be back down."

"You're staying in?" I asked.

"Yeah, I have some business to take care of, but you know you're more important. I'll have Josh take care of it for me," he said, walking away.

Hearing my brother say that brought a slight smile to my face. No matter what was going on in my life, I could always count on my brother to come through. That's why I never question anything that he asks of me. I learned that the hard way when I chose to live with Jermaine's family instead of him.

I still remembered how betrayed my brother felt. That is the one thing in my life that if I could do it differently, I would.

Twenty minutes later, Montez came down the stairs and joined us. He didn't drink Patrón so he grabbed his bottle of D'ussé. He started pouring shot after shot. He looked like he needed this liquid poison more than I did. I knew he had a lot on his mind and no one to talk to about it. It wasn't like he could tell me and Myra what was going on in the streets because it would put our lives at risk.

About an hour later, one of the guards was bringing the food in. Montez had ordered some pizzas, hot wings, garlic bread, and a salad. I'm guessing he's about to feed his crew because there's no way we can eat all of this shit.

We made our plates then spent the rest of the night drinking, eating, and smoking. We reminisced about how times were when our father was alive and how we thought our lives would be if he was still here. I know for a fact all of us would be living a different path if he was still here. Well, maybe all of us except Stephen, because he was always on dumb shit. He was the only rebellious one of the group. The rest of us aimed to make our father happy.

Montez would be a lawyer right now for one of those big fancy firms. Kiana would probably still be a teacher but she would also have a close relationship with us. Myra would be a juvenile counselor. As for me, I would be finishing up my criminal justice degree because I wanted to follow my big brother's footsteps. It's like my father's death changed the lives of all of his kids, baby mamas, and the people around him.

Eventually, Josh showed up at the house to discuss business with Montez , and I was getting tired so I headed upstairs to shower. Stripping out of my clothes, I climbed in the shower and allowed the hot water to wash away my pain. The tears and sadness hit me like a bag of rocks. Thoughts of the past came flowing back to me. There were so many red flags in my life that I ignored.

When you're in the midst of loving a man, you never take heed to the warning signs and what the people around you are telling you. It can be your mother, brother, father, sister, grandparents, or your best friend. Your first thought is that your family doesn't want to see you happy or that they're jealous because they're not in your situation. There's no way that the man you've chosen to have kids with and build a future with could do the things that they're telling you. There were so many red flags about my relationship that I ignored because I loved this man. He was home every night and he provided for me and our daughter in the beginning. He showed me unconditional love and I was genuinely happy.

My sister and brother tried to warn me about him from day one, but I ignored them. Hell, his own sister tried to warn me about his ass. That alone should have said a lot. They all tried to warn me that I was too good for him, but I couldn't see it. It wasn't that I thought they would steer me wrong, because I loved them more than anything. A lot of it had to do with the fact that I gave that man four years of my life and he was my first everything.

It was my own insecurities that allowed me to fall in love with Jermaine. I had built a guard around my heart and all it took was whispers of sweet nothings for my barriers to come crumbling down for him. If I had known what I knew now, I would have walked away at the first 'hello beautiful.' I just couldn't resist his charms and now I was paying for the shit.

I was infatuated with thoughts of loving him. I was willing to turn a blind eye to all of the bullshit. When you look up the word infatuated, it means to be possessed by an unreasonable passion or attraction. Love is the most spectacular, indescribable, deep, euphoric feeling for someone. Therefore, infatuated with love means to be in love with the idea of being in love. To assume you're in love without a proper reason. You're giving a man the opportunity to destroy you but trusting with your heart that he won't do it. Boy was I wrong this time.

Finding out your man is cheating through a text or phone call is one thing, but when you see the shit with your own eyes, it hurts like hell. There's no excuse seeing another woman riding your man's dick, and in your bed at that. They better be lucky I didn't pull a Burning Bed on their ass. All the things he told me I would never have to worry about all happened in the same day. I was getting tired of thinking about this shit. It all was becoming depressing as hell.

I finished washing up then climbed out of the shower. I brushed my teeth and put on my robe before leaving out of the bathroom. Josh was coming out of the other bathroom across the hall. His eyes roamed my body and the small silk robe I had on left little to the imagination. On any other day I would have just walked in my room and paid him no attention, but I was hurting. I motioned for him to follow me in my room and he did so.

As soon as he walked in, I closed and locked the door before crashing my lips into his. His hands roamed my body and my robe dropped to the floor. Lifting me off my feet, he placed me on the bed and placed gentle kisses down my body until he made it to my honey pot. He licked and sucked on my clit, causing me to grip the bed sheets. It felt like he was spelling Josh into my pussy. This nigga had my toes curling as I arched my back. I thought Jermaine's head was good because I never had anything to compare it to. Now I couldn't wait to see what some other dick felt like. Josh ate my pussy until I came like three times. I was ready for him to get undressed so we could fuck, but he never took his clothes off.

"You feel better now?" he asked.

"Yeah, but I'd feel even better if you took your clothes off and fucked me," I replied.

"I'm not going to fuck you Mercedes, at least not right now. If circumstances was different and you asked for the dick, I would give it to you, but not like this. I know that you're sad and drunk right now. I don't want you to wake up in the morning and regret anything. I only ate your pussy to help calm you down so you can get some sleep. I'll see you tomorrow, beautiful," he said, walking away.

I slightly pouted as I climbed out of the bed. I know I should be happy that he respected me like this but at the same time, I wanted some dick too. I guess the three orgasms would have to do. Before I knew it, I was on my side passed out, sleeping like a baby.

CHAPTER ELEVEN
MARIO (RIO)

Over the past three months, my life has changed since Mercedes entered it. She was someone that I never thought I needed to know. Her personality and vibe was different from what I was used to dealing with. When I met her in the club I just thought she was fine as fuck and we could have a little bit of fun. As I got to know her and learned her story, all I wanted to do was protect her.

My day-to-day life is hectic as hell. I'm a twenty-eight-year-old kingpin that works aside my thirty-year-old brother, Max. My father started grooming us each when we turned thirteen years old. It was like our gift and rite of passage. By the time I was fourteen I knew how to weigh dope and was a sharpshooter. We continued training until we were eighteen. He didn't care if we went to college but we definitely had to finish high school. When my father was ready to sit down, I was twenty-one years old. Since Max was older he had the option to be at the top, but he declined and decided to work up under me. He was older but I was better at this shit.

Back then Max was young and dumb. He didn't care about

how the business actually ran. All he wanted to do was kill people and get money, so I let him do him. I was happy to be at the top. I loved the fuck out of what I was doing. Do you know how much pussy you get running an empire at twenty-one years old? Nobody could tell me shit. I had bad bitches, money, cars, and houses. I had shit that I didn't even need. I was becoming too flashy and my father had to pull me to the side and talk to me. He told me at the rate I was going, I was either going to be dead by thirty, in jail, or broke. I needed to start making smarter decisions, and that's what I did.

Now that we're older, Max has changed as well. He wants to be included more in the decision process and I'm cool with that. We built our organization in Miami but we're looking into expanding. ATL was at the top of my list, which is why I was there the night of Bryce's party. My plan was to go scope out the competition and then move in on it.

I hit up Bryce and told him what I wanted to do. That's when he told me we should talk in person, so I took that trip. He advised me that wouldn't be a good idea because of Tez. At first I was ready to say fuck Tez, until I met him and saw he was a laid back nigga. Even though he was the boss, he still treated everybody as equals. He wasn't demanding or tossing his name around. He acted like an ordinary nigga and I respected that.

I decided to do things the right way and had Bryce arrange a meeting with us because I didn't want to end up in a turf war with him. That would make it difficult to get his sister to like me. I also just didn't want unnecessary problems. I'm almost thirty years old, and by that time I plan on settling down and having more kids. In order for me to do that, I have to grind hard over these next couple years. I don't need to worry about looking over my shoulder.

A week later I had a meeting with Tez. I discussed my plan

of expanding with him and he said he was also looking into expanding as well, so we came to a common ground. He'd allow me to open up business in a certain spot of his area and vice versa. We also discussed starting a legitimate business together. He already has his father's studio and I wanted to run a record label, so we could make something happen. Even though Tez was only a couple years older than me I knew I could learn a lot from him. I respected the fact that he got to where he was on his own.

Before we signed any paperwork, I told him up front that I liked his sister and planned on pursuing her. I was a grown ass man and I wasn't about to sneak around with her or hide. That shit was bad for business off rip. He didn't really like that idea because, I mean, who would want their baby sister dating a kingpin? He did know that I could protect her and provide for her if it ever came down to that. His only request was to keep my personal life with his sister away from our business, which was understandable and something I could handle.

Originally Max was going to be the one to go to ATL and get everything started, but after talking with my pops we thought it was better for him to stay here since everything was already set up. He wasn't sure if Max was ready to build on his own. I was cool with that because it gave me more time to get to know Mercedes better, plus Max has like five kids out here and I only have one.

Pulling my suitcase from my closet, I started packing for the week. Right now I've been splitting my time between Atlanta and Miami, but I plan on changing that soon. Once I have everything up and running in Atlanta, I'm going to tell Max he can have Miami. I'll just come back for important meetings or if he needs help with something. I already told my girl Yasmine my plans and she needed to figure out what she wanted to do.

"Rio, you're leaving already? You just got here two days ago," Yasmine said from behind me.

"I know, but I told you it was going to be like this for a minute. It takes a lot of work to build something new in a state that you don't live in."

"I know, it's just that I miss you and I need some money. I want to go out with my girls tonight," she replied.

I knew that's what this was all about. She don't give a fuck if I'm in town or not as long as I leave her some money. We've been together off and on for the past six years and it's always the same thing. She loves the idea of being with me but she couldn't care less about loving me. She's used to the luxury lifestyle I provide for her.

I met Yasmine at this party a year after I took over. Back then I wasn't looking at women for their personalities. I was simply adding them to the roster just off of looks. She was a bad bitch to me so I wanted and approached her. She was a light-skinned thick chick with big lips. My first thought was her lips looked like they could do wonders.

We started fucking around and she got pregnant. I didn't really want a relationship but I decided to give it a try because of the baby. Our relationship lasted for about a year after my daughter was born, then we broke up because she wanted to be a bad bitch first and a mother second. My mother told me she didn't know why I was surprised. I knew the kind of woman she was before we started dating. I was thankful for my mother because she's the one that helped me take care of my daughter, Yris.

When my daughter turned three, Yasmine decided she wanted to stop running the streets and come back to be a mother. Well, at least that's the lie she told me. When I took her back I told her shit was going to be different. My parents would keep Yris during the weekends and she could roam the streets all she wants, but Sunday through Friday she had to be a mother. She agreed and that only lasted for a few months until she got back to her old ways. At that point I was like fuck it and let her do whatever she wanted.

Yasmine and I don't have a traditional relationship. We both agreed that it would be best for us to have an open relationship because we continued to cheat on each other. The shit was toxic as hell. She'd find out I cheated and get to busting bitches' windows out, and I'd find out she cheated and put her out. It went on and on like that for almost a year until I was like fuck it. You do you and I do me.

We did have a few rules though. We can't bring the other person we're fucking with to the house we shared. We can't go in public with them where our friends and family would see them together, and we can't have them around our daughter. She's four years old and we don't need to be confusing her.

At first I was fine with what we have going on because I was able to do me either way and that's what mattered. However, after meeting Mercedes, I know that things are going to have to change. I'm going to eventually have to leave Yasmine alone. I just have to figure out how to do it without it affecting my daughter. Yasmine can be manipulative and vindictive at times. I would hate to have to kill her for playing with me about my daughter, because she knows I will do anything for her.

"I'll drop Yris off at my mama's house on the way to the airport and transfer you some money," I finally said.

"Okay, thank you baby. I'm about to go to the mall now. Have a safe trip," she replied, running out of the room, proving my point.

If I lived in a perfect world, Yasmine would have waited and gave me a kiss. Begged me to dick her down because she was going to miss me being gone for a week. Waited until I was finished packing to see if I needed anything before I left. I guess that's the thing though. My life is far from perfect so I take what I can get. Hell, I can't even remember the last time I had sex with Yasmine and that's fucked up. It definitely says a lot about our relationship. Open relationship or not, we're both supposed to still want to do stuff with each other, but that's simply not the case.

I finished packing my suitcase then got Yris together and left the house. I hurriedly drove to my parents' house. I only had enough time to say hi before I had to drive across town to the airport so I wouldn't miss my flight. Once I landed, I took an Uber home. Since I was still getting adjusted to being out here, I'm renting a mansion for a year and then I'll probably buy something later. I want to see how everything goes before I make that kind of commitment.

I sent Mercedes a message letting her know that I'll pick her up in about an hour, before I went in the bathroom to take a quick shower. I was looking forward to spending time with her. Every day with her is like coming up for fresh air. The way I was feeling about her is how you're supposed to feel when you're in a relationship with someone.

The thing is, we're not in a relationship though. We do everything that people do in a relationship just without the title. That's mainly because of her though. I told her that we would do everything at her pace and I meant it. I know she's dealing with some shit and I'm a patient man. I'm not going to pressure her into being with me right now because I have my own shit to get in order, but once that's taken care of, it's over with. I'm locking her down and she's not going to go anywhere. I'm going to do everything in my power to make it where she wouldn't even want to if she could.

CHAPTER TWELVE
MERCEDES

Looking down at my phone, a huge smile spread across my face when I saw Rio's message. It had only been two days since I last saw him, but I missed him. My situation with Rio is different from my relationship with Jermaine. Rio is understanding and not trying to rush me into anything. Everything that has happened between us has been at my pace. From the first time we kissed to the first time we had sex. He knows that I'm not ready to start a new relationship yet. I like Rio a lot but after what happened with Jermaine, I'm scared to give another man my heart right now.

The thing I like most about Rio is that he doesn't try to shelter me or keep me in a box. He takes me out in the world and allows me to enjoy life. He allows me to be young, wild, and free without consequences. For the first time in my life, I'm actually able to do whatever makes me happy without having to consider someone else's feelings. I'm starting to live the life that a twenty-one-year-old should have.

I've learned so much from Rio in just the few months that I've known him. He's not just a street nigga. He's smart as hell and I think I like him so much because he reminds me of Montez . He's been helping me get everything I need in order to start my own business. I'll still be working at the construction company but I wanted to do more. I'm going to open an online boutique but instead of just selling clothes, I'm going to sell hair, shoes, and jewelry as well. I've already started the process of getting some custom shoes designed. I told Rio my ideas of how I wanted the sandals, gym shoes, and heels to look. I was going to hire somebody to draw out the designs for me but Rio surprised me and did them for me himself.

The fifty thousand dollars that Jermaine had in his safe was being put to good use. I used some of the money for lipo and a boob job. The rest of the money was going to fund my business. A week after everything happened, I decided not to be a bitch. I looked up lawyers and found one. The morning of the meeting where I was going to give them the money, Tori called me talking crazy about how I had no business keeping his money. I wasn't about to argue with her because I had already made the decision to do what he asked me to with it, so I hung up on her.

The bitch just couldn't leave well enough alone. She sent me a text message telling me that she was four months pregnant with his baby. Just that quick after reading that, she had fucked it up for him and I decided I was going to use the money how I wanted. I called AT&T immediately after and changed my phone number. At that point, him or his family no longer existed to me.

I stayed with Montez for two months until things calmed down and then I moved into my own house. He wanted to buy me one but I'm not ready to be a homeowner yet, so he's renting me one that's less than five minutes from him. He paid the rent up for a year until I decide what I want. I would have stayed with him longer but since I'm dating Rio, I wanted him to have an actual address to pick me up from instead of me always having to drive and meet him places. I wanted the full dating experience. Pick me up from my house and drop me back off. Walk me to the front door and kiss me goodnight, and he does all of that.

I took a quick shower since time wasn't on my side, then got dressed in a short black skater dress with a pair of black sandals that tied around my legs. I brushed my hair up into a ponytail and put on my everyday jewelry which consisted of my hoop and stud earrings, a silver cross chain, tennis bracelet, and a heart ring. Just as I was applying my lip gloss, Rio sent a message saying he was outside. I finished what I was doing and grabbed my purse before going out to meet him.

A smile spread across my face when I saw his sexy ass leaning up against his car. He pulled me into a hug and I melted at the scent of his cologne. He released me from the hug and kissed me softly on the lips before stepping away.

"Hello, beautiful," he spoke, opening the car door for me.

"Hey there, handsome," I replied as I got inside of the car.

Rio ran around to his side of the car and got in.

"You can change the music to whatever you want," he told me as he pulled off.

Once we were out of the residential area, Rio started driving fast as hell, as usual.

"Rio, slow down before you give me whiplash," I screeched.

"Relax baby, I know I have precious cargo in the car with me." He smirked, looking in my direction and causing me to blush. Little comments like that is what's causing me to fall for this man more and more each passing day.

We went and had dinner at Fin's and Feathers. It was a nice spot that I had never been to. The food and drinks were amazing. It was Karaoke night, so I enjoyed that. We didn't go on stage to sing but we did sing along from our seat with everyone that was on stage. We stayed for about an hour and a half when he got a call that they needed him at the trap. He offered to take me home but he had just got here and I didn't want the night to end, so I rode with him.

When we made it there I told him I'd sit in the car, but he wasn't having that. Being that it was a trap house, it was in a not-so-great neighborhood. Anything could happen and he wanted me to remain safe. We got out of the car and he held my hand as we walked in the house. Some of the guys just looked at me and the ones that knew me through Tez spoke. I was glad as hell that I wasn't sneaking around because I know they gone tell my brother they saw me with Rio.

Surprisingly, Montez is okay with me dating Rio. It could be because him and Rio are cool. Rio is also the exact opposite of Jermaine. He has his head on his shoulders and he's stable. I thought the issue would be because he's a street nigga, but all he told me was to be careful. I'm grown now and he only wants to see me happy. I know that he will be there if I need him to step in, but so far I haven't.

I sat down in one of the back rooms while Rio handled his business in the front with the guys. Whatever was going on must not have been major because we left about forty minutes later.

"Do you want to go back to my place or yours?" Rio asked as he pulled off.

"We can go back to yours. My sister is keeping Kayla tonight for me."

During the drive to Rio's house, I noticed him looking back and forth between the mirror and the road.

"Mercedes, get that key out of the arm rest and get that gun out of my glove compartment."

I looked behind us and saw two black cars, so I hurriedly did as I was told.

Bow, Bow, Bow

Suddenly, loud gunshots filled the air and bullets started hitting the car.

"What the fuck?" I yelled.

Rio rolled down the driver's side window and let off some shots as he drove.

"I can't drive and shoot at the same time. I'm going to need you to shoot so I can concentrate on us not crashing."

"Rio, I've never shot at anyone before," I said.

"I know baby, but I've seen you at the range. You know what you're doing, so come on before we end up dying tonight," he told me, swerving the car through traffic.

I took my seat belt off and rolled down the window. I had to lean halfway out of the window as I started firing shots back. As I was shooting, Rio was driving fast as hell. A couple of minutes later, he had lost them and I put the gun back where I got it from.

"You did good ma." He smiled, looking at me as if we weren't just in a shootout.

"I did good, Rio? Are you serious? What the hell is going on? Why are we being shot at?"

"I don't know, baby. I honestly don't think this has to do with me. I haven't been out here long enough to have beef with anybody. Once we're a little further away, I'm going to have to call your brother."

"Okay, can we just go to my house instead? I'd be more comfortable there after what just happened."

I lived in a gated community where you needed to put in a code to get through the gates and I had around-the-clock security at my house. Tez had one of his guys parked in my driveway at all times, even when I'm not at home.

"Alright, but you're with me and I'm not going to ever let anything happen to you. I'm capable of taking care of you, but I understand you being scared right now," he said, driving to my house.

By the time we made it to my house, Bryce, Josh, and Tez were already there sitting in my living room. Me, Myra, and Montez always kept a key to each other's houses for safety reasons. When Tez saw me, he pulled me into a tight hug and just held me for a minute before releasing and examining me.

"Are you alright?" he asked.

"Yeah, just a little shaken up," I admitted.

"What happened?" Montez asked, looking at Rio.

I could tell something was going on that I didn't know about and that I probably didn't need to know about, so I excused myself and went inside of the kitchen so they could talk. I grabbed a bottle of water from the refrigerator and sat at the island. I was lost in my thoughts when Josh sat down next to me.

"You good?" Josh asked me.

"Yeah, it just all caught me off guard. How are you?"

"I'm doing good. You know me, out here taking care of business and watching your brother's back, as usual. Rio told us how you handled yourself. Your brother is proud as hell of you," he said, causing me to smile.

Josh and I continued talking for a little while longer until Tez called me. Ever since that night Josh gave me head, we've grown closer. Not on no relationship type of stuff but more as friends. He knows that I have something going on with Rio so he stopped flirting and coming on to me. It's so funny that he respects what I have going on with somebody that I'm not in a relationship with but didn't respect my four-year relationship. I guess everybody except me just knew Jermaine was not the one for me.

I talked to Tez for a few minutes before he left. He had to go take care of some business and figure out who was shooting at us. Bryce needed to talk to Rio about something, so I went upstairs to my bedroom and got undressed then climbed into bed.

Rio came walking in the room fifteen minutes later and just stared at my naked body for what felt like eternity before he took off his clothes and joined me.

"You ready for me to tuck you in, ma?" he whispered in my ear.

"Yes I am, daddy," I purred. Calling a man daddy was definitely something new to me. I had never in my life called Jermaine that shit because he didn't give daddy vibes. Now Rio, on the other hand, gave daddy and big dick energy vibes.

I nodded my head before he crashed his lips into mine. My fingers went from rubbing his head to his back as the kiss intensified. This man had my pussy wet as hell and all he did was kiss me.

"I swear you're so fucking beautiful," he told me, breaking our kiss and looking directly in my eyes.

My body tingled at his touch. Skipping over my honey pot, he kissed my inner thighs before spreading my legs and diving into my sweet juices, almost sending me up the wall. My moans filled the room.

Grabbing the back of his head, I pushed him farther into me as I arched my back, nearing my climax. Not being able to take any more, I tried to push away but the hold he had on me wouldn't allow me to move. Unable to hold back anymore, I reached my peak, grabbing and holding onto his head. Rio didn't stop there he kept going, gently nibbling and licking, causing me to climax again. He came up for air, kissing me on my lips, allowing me to taste myself before laying down on his back.

Leaning down, I licked his dick like a lollipop before placing it in my mouth. Moving my head up and down, I used my hands to stroke him. Alternating between fast and slow. He grabbed the back of my head and started to face fuck me. I was so glad that my reflexes were on point, because he was bigger than Jermaine. It felt like I was going to choke on Rio's dick the first time I gave him head.

I stopped giving him head for a minute and grabbed a Magnum from my nightstand. Opening it up, I slid it on his dick before switching positions. Climbing on top of me, he took his time sliding inside of me.

"Mmhhmm," I moaned in his ear.

"Damn babe, you feel good as hell," he whispered as he slowly stroked me. He had to take his time because I was still getting used to his nine-inch dick. Not only was it nine inches, the girth was thick as hell. He began thrusting in and out of me until I came. He rolled over on his back and I caught my breath before climbing on top of him and riding in reverse cowgirl.

"Fuck Rio, I'm about to cum again," I announced as I twerked on his dick.

"Damn Cedes," he moaned as he smacked me on the ass.

Rio and I fucked for about an hour before his body tensed up and he came inside of the condom. The sex between us was amazing and I could only imagine how it would be without a condom. I'm not going there yet anytime soon though, even though I'm on birth control. I'm not fucking a man raw again until I'm in love.

We got up and took a shower before climbing back in bed. He laid on his side and I slid my body into his before closing my eyes and falling right to sleep. The following morning, I woke up to Rio sliding his dick inside of me. We got our morning session out of the way and then took a quick shower. We were going to have breakfast then go pick up Makayla and go to the mall. After that he said we can do whatever I want. He took the day off to spend it with me Kayla.

Rio was always making sure to include Makayla in things but also made sure we had our adult time as well. He definitely knew how to play the stepdaddy role. At first I was skeptical about having her around him but then I thought, what the hell. I did plan on getting into a relationship with him so he was going to be around her regardless.

CHAPTER THIRTEEN
JERMAINE

It's been almost three months since I got locked up. I've been sitting in Rice County Jail awaiting my trial. I declined the plea deal and was hoping for a miracle. They've denied me bail twice already. Talking about I'm a fucking flight risk. I have no idea where they got that thought from since I don't have any money. Like, this entire situation is straight bullshit. They're trying to get me to take a plea deal for eight years. It would be for the drug and gun charge. One of my bullets did hit somebody but they didn't die, or my sentencing would be worse. I've been debating on taking the deal or not.

The lawyer I have is shitty as hell but better than a public defender. Had Mercedes not fucked me over I could have had a better lawyer and probably been able to get bail. I can't complain though, because this was who my mama, Kelly, and Tori could afford. They put their money together to look out for me.

Tori was stressing about what she was going to do now that she didn't have my help. She couldn't afford the house on her own, so my mother agreed to let her move in with her. She didn't really like her but she was pregnant with her grandchild. Tori was happy about that because she didn't want to have to raise our baby on the streets.

After the fight Tori threatened to press charges against Mercedes but I had to convince her not to. I ended up coming clean about my relationship because at this point, there was no need to lie. It wasn't like I was going to be with either one of them anytime soon anyway. It's not like Cedes did real damage to her. All she did was hit her in the face a few times. Even if she did more I still wouldn't let her press charges against her. It's crazy how Mercedes all but left me for dead in here and I still love her. All I ever wanted is what's best for her. I can't have the mother of my child in jail behind me fucking up. No one can love or take care of our daughter better than her mother can.

The guard announced that it was visiting time. I climbed out of my bunk and put on my shoes before leaving my cell. I got in the single file line and waited for them to pat me down before going to the visiting area. I sat down behind the thick ass glass and picked up the phone at the same time as Tori. I told her that she didn't have to keep coming to visit me but she insisted. I just knew she was going to run for the hills after finding out the truth about me and Mercedes, but she didn't. She said she was going to stick by my side even if we're just friends so that I could have a part in my child's life.

I respected the hell out of her for that. I'm not sure how long that will last though, because if I take this plea deal I'll be getting shipped right up out of here and to a new state. I need to get somebody to convince Mercedes to bring Makayla here. I want to at least get the chance to make amends with her before it's too late.

"Hey baby, how are you doing?" Tori spoke.

"I'm hanging in there, how's our son doing?"

"He's doing good. He be kicking his ass off. Your mama told me to tell you hi and that she'll be here to visit you on Thursday."

"Okay, good looking out. Did she say anything about Mercedes?"

"She said to tell you that Mercedes still isn't answering your calls. Kelly went over to the house a week after you got locked up and everything was gone. The building manager said she told them to take the damages for the door out of her security deposit and to Zelle her the rest of the money. She didn't leave a forwarding address or anything."

"Damn, okay. I'm sorry if this is awkward for you to talk to me about her. I just really want a chance to see my daughter before I go to prison. It's bad enough she's going to have to grow up without me."

"You don't have to apologize to me for wanting to be a father. It's not your fault that your baby mama is being a bitch," she replied.

"It actually is my fault. I met Mercedes when she was seventeen years old. She was naive and vulnerable at the time. I molded her into the perfect woman I wanted and when she became that woman, I didn't know how to handle it. I put that girl through hell and she stayed by my side. I was down to my last and she tried her best to help me build. All I had to do was watch our daughter and I couldn't do that," I explained. I wasn't about to sit around and allow anybody to bad mouth Mercedes. My mama and Kelly not even mad at her for what she did. All they want is to be able to spend time with Kayla.

I believe Mercedes just needs some time to clear her head and get over the hurt, then she'll come around because she loves my mom and sister. She's probably feeling like they betrayed her. In her mind, for all she know, they knew about Tori the entire time, which wasn't the case.

"Why are you always defending her? I'm the one coming out here every Saturday to see you. She ran off with fifty thousand dollars of your money and all you can say is damn, that's fucked up."

"I defend her because she's not here to defend herself. She never knew anything about you. She gave me opportunity after opportunity to tell her the truth and I didn't. If someone was talking about you or calling you a bitch, I would defend you as well."

"You're right, I just hate the way you still love her. I'm doing everything I can to be here for you and put money on your books and it still feels like it isn't enough," she said.

"Enough for what, Tori? It's not like you can buy the love I have for her and transfer it over to you. I was with that girl four years and we went through major shit together. That don't change just because I started liking you. The timing of it all is just fucked up. You have to see things from her point of view. Imagine you was in love with a man, helping him get back on his feet, only to know he was starting something new with someone else. You also have to remember she's only twenty-one."

"Okay, I'll stop talking about it. I just hate that you're still in here because of her."

"I mean, yes and no. There was no guarantee that I was going to get bonded out, and I'm sure once she calms down she's going to give me my money back. She's not a bad person."

"You sure do have a lot of confidence in her. I'm sure that money is long gone now," Tori replied.

I shrugged my shoulders because I didn't want to talk about the money or Mercedes anymore. I changed the subject and asked her about her doctor's appointments. Her face lit up as she talked about that. She was happy as hell to be mother and I can tell. I just hate that she's going to go through it alone. I know my mother and sister will help the best way they can, but that's not the same.

I finished up my visit with Tori and went back to my cell. My cell is where I spend most of my time. I don't go to yard or hang out anywhere here. I'm in maximum security with real killers that don't have shit to lose. I was outside fooling myself because this lifestyle is not for me. I was kidding myself the entire time, doing dumb shit for no reason. My ass should have just got a job like Mercedes told me to. Instead, I wanted to live the fast life and prove her brother wrong when he wasn't even paying attention to me at all.

My everyday routine consisted of eating, working out, and reading. My cell mate has been teaching me chess and I'm actually enjoying learning it. It takes a lot of patience, which was something that I originally lacked. Now I have nothing but patience and time here.

They announced chow time so I left my cell and went to the cafeteria. I grabbed my tray with some runny mashed potatoes and an unidentifiable meat with a small hot fruit punch. They were feeding us shit I wouldn't even feed my dog. I looked around and walked over to my usual table. I held my head down and ate my food. I figured as long as I keep to myself, nobody will bother me, and that seems to have been working for the past few months. I know once I get to prison it will be different, depending on where they take me.

I finished up my meal and put my tray away. They only gave us seven minutes to eat because they had to get us out and get the next batch in. Whenever I get out of here I know I'm going straight and narrow. There is no way I can endure this again. I also know that it's going to get worse before it can get better.

As I was walking to my cell, it felt like someone was

watching me. This is jail and we're in here packed like sardines, so, of course, someone is watching me. I brushed my paranoia off and went back in my cell. I was about to climb in my bunk when I felt somebody hit me in the back of my head.

"What the fuck," I groaned, turning around.

There were two big ass, Van Diesel type of niggas that looked like they were up to no good.

"Look, I don't want any problems," I said, raising my hand.

The guys just looked at me and laughed before they started beating my ass. I'm talking about they were punching me in my face and all over my body. Even when I was on the ground they started kicking me. The kicks were so hard I could feel my ribs cracking. I was in so much pain that I couldn't even cry, and people just stood around watching me get beat half to death. It would have been nice to know what I was getting my ass kicked for. Eventually I zoned out and awaited my death, but it never came. One of the guys squatted down so he could be certain I heard him.

"Tez says hi," were the only words he spoke before walking away, leaving me battered and bruised. The only thing that came to mind was I was fucked, before I passed out.

To Be Continued....

AUTHOR NOTES

I would like to thank everyone that has supported part one of my new series. I appreciate all of the support that is shown to me. Without you all I wouldn't be where I am now. I love getting feedback from you all so please leave an honest review. It doesn't matter if you loved or hated the book. Reviews help us figure out what can we improve in our work. It's like report cards for authors.

I love to stay connected with my readers so feel free to reach out.

Follow me on Facebook: Author Kevina Hopkins

Twitter: @vina2006

Instagram: Author Kevina Hopkins

Email: kevinahopkinspresents@gmail.com

For sneak peeks, contests and details on upcoming release join my Facebook group.

https://www.facebook.com/groups/310317121338672

ALSO BY KEVINA HOPKINS

When A Savage Loves A Woman 2

The Autobiography Of A Capo's Wife

Every Dope Boy Got A Side Chick

Made in the USA
Monee, IL
03 October 2023